COLD TURKEY

SWEET AS MAPLE SYRUP

BOOK TWO

ID JOHNSON

For Watts

CONTENTS

CHAPTER 1

Cally

THE FRAGRANT ONIONS SIZZLE IN THE PAN, MAKING MY MOUTH WATER. My stomach gurgles in annoyance. I give it a gentle pat and say, "Just fifteen more minutes," reaching through the industrial-sized refrigerator door and grabbing another pound of hamburger and some lettuce, ignoring my fussy tummy until my lunch break.

My parents' restaurant, Maple Falls Café, has been very busy today. I've been assisting in the kitchen, bustling around getting the orders cooked, plated, and to the serving window, while secretly adding a little extra pizzazz to a dish once in a while.

It's not that the food is bad, but I like to have fun with it, and while I'm working here, I'm limited to my parents' recipes. Most of my cooking is done after hours or in my kitchen, and there, I have the freedom to experiment.

"Cally Stein, you know we don't put cilantro in that," my dad cautions me from the stove.

I yank my hand back from the soup cup I'm about to put in the serving window and spin around, shoving the cilantro down into the front of my apron pocket. "What cilantro?" I try to say innocently.

My dad suppresses a laugh and shakes his head. "Sweetie, I know you think your versions are better, and I'll admit that you've got good taste, but people don't want to be surprised here," he says in his soulful voice. "My recipes haven't changed in ten years, hun. Changing things now could break the town's trust."

My shoulders slump. I know it's the truth. Maple Falls Café is known for its dependable taste and familiar menu. My dad is the main cook, and he's kind but strict when it comes to following his recipes. I've been helping him since I was fifteen and know how to make every item on the menu by heart. But I really enjoy cooking, and I want to share some of my creations once in a while.

I roll my shoulders and strengthen my resolve. "What about the seasonal dish menu we talked about? Have you thought about it? I can make some samples for you. I have a lot of good ideas—"

My dad raises his hand and turns back to his soup pot. "We'll talk about it later," he says. "Let's get through this rush first."

I peek through the serving window and note that almost every single booth and table is full. I'm amazed that my dad can do all this cooking by himself most days, since our other cooks are part time. I've been pretty much full time since getting my culinary degree, but we don't always work the same shift.

Jarred and Andrea, our servers, zip through their sections, topping off drinks and passing out receipts. My mother, Cara, is manning the register, seating new customers, and handling the cashiering. Mom is the face of Maple Falls Café. The place was born of my father's desire, but my mom keeps it afloat. And I… do what I can here and there and try to help.

Fifteen minutes turn into thirty when a group of ten teachers comes in. Several of them look the same as they did when I left high school eight years ago. One of my former classmates is actually among them—Jen. This must be her second year teaching high school. Why she wanted to return there is a million-dollar question to me. I remember how excited we all were to graduate and spend our days somewhere else, finally.

When I finally get to take a quick break, I hang my patchwork apron on a hook on the wall by the swinging door and meet my mom behind the register. She's just finished ringing up the recently retired Maple Falls Tour Company owner, Mr. Randal Seeley, and his wife, Margie. I wave hello before they leave, and Mr. Seeley shares his signature radiant smile.

"You doing okay?" I ask my mom, moving her long black ponytail off her shoulder so it hangs down her back. I note the little beads of sweat on the nape of her neck.

"I'm good, sweetie," she says, rubbing a couple of quick circles on my back. "You taking a break?"

I look out at the bustling restaurant, the large group of teachers seated in the middle. Several of the tables look close to finishing.

"Nah," I say. "I came to relieve you for a bit. Dad, uh, wants your opinion on something in the back. Something about a supply order, maybe?"

My mother squints at me, but it seems like she's taking my word for it, so I place my hands on her shoulders and guide her toward the back.

"Yeah, yeah," I continue. "It was definitely about the next supply order. Feel free to take your time, and I'll take over here for a little bit."

My mother sighs. "I don't know why this couldn't wait until later," she grumbles.

Since I've managed to trick my mother into taking a break, I do my part, ringing up the group of teachers and a couple of other tables who have finished their food. When she returns about twenty minutes later, I go back to helping my father in the kitchen until we close.

Dad lets me fix the three of us a late dinner in the cafe kitchen. Since our restaurant is more of a diner than a fancy restaurant, there are limited ingredients. I manage to whip together a recipe I have been trying to get my dad to add as a specialty or seasonal item: loaded chili dogs, with Amoroso rolls split at the top and slightly hollowed out to accommodate more filling, smoky-flavored grilled hotdogs, and sweet chili topped with salty crushed corn nuts and spicy jalapeños. For a personalized taste, I prepare some cucumber radish and sour cream.

I wanted to come up with a cute name for them, but I'd given up after my dad turned down my last couple of ideas. What can I say? He's a man of tradition. He knows what has worked for him so far, and he doesn't want to "mess up perfection," as he puts it.

While I'm cooking, my parents get started on redecorating the restaurant, taking down the skeletons, jack-o'-lanterns, and black felt cats. Halloween is over now, and, as always, it was a lot of fun!

I was happy to see Meena, my cousin, dress up as her favorite video game character Ha-nana, since last year she bailed on that idea and opted to be a princess like her friends. It seems like she's slowly becoming her own person and letting that shine. I'm happy for her. My quirky little wind-up doll costume totally slayed. But as much as I enjoy Halloween, Thanksgiving gives me life–the food is its crowning glory!

We eat the loaded chili dogs as a family in one of the booths, making small talk about my older siblings, who have all moved on and left this restaurant and town behind.

My mother makes a couple of comments about how tasty the dinner is, and my dad simply nods in agreement. After eating our fill, we dedicate the next two hours to decking out the restaurant with little golden turkeys and cornucopias, leaves and acorns, and various squashes and gourds.

By the end of it, my mind is swirling with ideas for new recipes to try for our family meal. It's only a few weeks away!

It's slow the next night, so I'm able to take a long dinner break when my best friend Autumn and her fiancé Lukas swing by the restaurant for dinner. I have to admit that I was very surprised at first that the two of them got together. I didn't know Lukas before because he is from out of town, but it was clear early on how smitten Autumn was with him.

Things were great with them at first—until she disassociated because he said he was going to move back to New York. But then he didn't, and he bought the tour company where she worked and gave it to her! It was a whole whirlwind affair if I've ever seen one!

But now, seeing them together over the last year, watching both of them come out of their shells and challenge each other and also comfort each other–man, that's what dreams are made of. My dreams, anyway....

"Wow! It's like fall threw up in here. I love it!" Autumn says. I know it's her way of praising the decor.

"Sweetheart, look." Lukas points out the waterfall of string lights in the bar area.

It's so sweet the way Autumn immediately turns to see what he's pointing at. Her green eyes take on a lovely glow as she studies the setup at the bar, with string lights and tendrils of leaves and pinecones. "Reminds me of the little gazebo in the middle of the fall festival where we got engaged," she croons, wrinkling her nose at him adorably.

He takes her hand and kisses the beautiful golden ring on her finger. It's so sweet, my stomach cinches up. I hope they will be this cute and happy forever.

And I hope I'm lucky enough to find a nice guy who loves me like that, one I can share my life with.

My heart aches a little, but I breathe out the pinching sensation with a puff of air and focus on my friends. "How's the wedding planning going?" I ask as we slide into a corner booth, with them on one side and me on the other.

They share a guilty look. "We haven't even started planning," they say simultaneously. Autumn shrugs her coat off her shoulders, and Lukas kindly folds it neatly beside him.

Ugh. I hate how much love these people right now. As a single girl, it's hard sometimes to be around them.

"Well, I hope you've at least decided who your maid of honor will be!" I tease.

Between Autumn owning and operating Maple Falls Tour Company and getting engaged, I haven't seen her much lately. We used to get together three or four times a week, and now it feels like it's three entire weeks since I've seen her. Plus, I love Lukas, too, but he's always here now. It might not be so bad if I had a guy of my own so we could double date, but I don't have anyone like that.

And not a single prospect.

We eat and chat for a couple of hours before Autumn tells me she's got to get to bed so she can wake up early to oversee a large group of tourists first thing in the morning. Lukas admits that he's exhausted from his earlier volleyball game and that he's ready to hit the hay, too. So, we wrap it up and say goodbye, parting ways like we don't know when we'll see each other again.

Since the cafe is still basically empty, my parents send me home. I start out on my walk home—four blocks south and another six blocks east to the little two-bedroom house I rent. The air is quiet and cold, and the sky is overcast with dimly moonlit clouds. T

he calm has my mind wandering. It suddenly strikes me how alone I feel without Autumn and without my parents. Even my other bestie, Ivy Dear, is working overtime at Hearthlight Inn, the bed and breakfast inn her parents own, with peak vacation season encroaching.

Everyone loves the fall colors in Maple Falls—especially the tourists.

My thoughts drift back to Autumn and Lukas. They're such a star couple. But as wonderful as it would be to have a charming man of my own, it's hard to imagine. I know every single man in this town, and everybody of marriageable age is already in a relationship, or they're just totally not my type.

Also, what even is my type? Maybe I haven't met anyone who fits it yet because I've always just been here. Maybe the only hope of me finding my other half is... leaving?

I gulp at the thought. I love Maple Falls. There's nowhere else I'd want to live.

Maybe I'll get lucky and have the perfect guy just show up here one day, just like what happened for Autumn.

A girl can dream.

CHAPTER 2

I hand my credit card to the driver and glance at my watch as he's processing the transaction. A lot of people call me crazy for not downloading all the ride-share apps or using my digital wallet for every little thing, but I guess I never bought into the idea. It might make things more time-efficient, but I hate shuffling through app after app to find the right one. I guess I'm just a traditional guy in that sense.

I glance down at my watch, thinking only for a split second that maybe having one of those apps might be worth it. But before the idea takes hold, my card is back in my hand, and I'm exiting the taxi with my satchel slung over my shoulder.

Chicago is indeed a windy city today, and the sky is a flat, slate gray, threatening us with snow soon. It's slightly too warm for that today, but the breeze breaks through my coat and my pants, sending a chill into my bones.

I make my way down the busy sidewalk and past the remnants of black and orange Halloween streamers, little bits of candy wrappers, and what is probably red fuzz from a devil costume's boa. I roll my eyes at the thought of people not caring where their trash ends up. They're usually more concerned with making it to the next party.

Inside Commers Communications's high-rise office building, the air thrums with activity—people skirting around each other, talking on their cellphones, and waiting for the elevator. I join the line waiting to head to the higher floors, and three more people come up behind me. When the doors open, I scan the crowd, dreading the next couple of minutes as the bodies all press together, and everyone's perfume and breakfast breath mingle in the confined space. The woman next to me leans into my arm, but I can't move away. My phone rings over and over in my pocket. I ignore it for now, not wanting to bump into anyone.

One of these days when I'm the CEO, I'll have my own private elevator up to a spacious office, where I'll make important decisions that move the company forward instead of being cramped in my little office all day long. I just have to get through this next presentation—oh, and the retirement of the current CEO, which probably won't take place for at least five years. But it's okay. I'm a patient person. I can handle the wait.

Ross Erkin, the current CEO who has worked here for at least twenty-five years, has made it clear he wants me to succeed him. He's been prepping me, slowly handing me greater responsibilities, complex projects, and more freedom. That doesn't mean I'm guaranteed the position, so I'm determined to prove myself in any way I can.

As the elevator stops floor by floor, the air becomes slightly more breathable. The woman next to me flicks a glance over her shoulder, tossing her brown curls over her shoulder as she exits, taking the overwhelming aroma of gardenias with her. Finally, the elevator dings on the thirtieth floor. I'm one of the last ones off.

"Mr. Thatcher!" my assistant Gloria calls, pressing on her desk and standing. "Good morning!"

She trots around on her short black heels, and as she has for the last six years, stands behind me and helps me shrug out of my coat. Gloria has been my assistant since I started here. She's been working here longer than me, and perhaps nearly as long as Mr. Erkin himself. She's a spindly, middle-aged woman with fine, textured curls and apple-like cheeks. And she's always in a good mood.

"Good morning, Gloria," I reply.

She folds my long coat over her arm and squeezes my shoulder. "You're feeling thin. I thought people were supposed to fatten up when winter's on the way!"

"You know I'm too busy to fatten up," I tell her, pressing my office door open. It's a pretty large office. I have a good ten feet of space on either side of my desk, as well as a separate seating area for less formal meetings. The view from the wall of windows shows a nice cityscape… usually. Today, it's bleak and gray. There's a haze looming close to the ground, and I'm not sure if it's fog or smog from all the car exhaust.

I sit at my desk and immediately get to work. As the current COO who is trying to prove myself worthy of the CEO position, I've taken the initiative to put together a presentation for Mr. Erkin to optimize workflows and highlight a few areas of improvement between departments. Only when we're self-actualized as a whole can we improve and retain customer satisfaction.

I get immersed in my work and finally glance up at the clock to see three hours have passed while I've been perfecting my presentation, though after getting sidetracked by emails and phone calls, I hardly feel like I've had time to do anything. Shaking my head, I get back to work. Just when I feel like I'm getting in a groove, Gloria knocks lightly on the door and peeks inside.

"You have a phone call," she says gently.

"Can you take a message? I'm just getting—"

"It's your mother," she says.

I let out a long sigh. My mom is probably just going to hound me about making time for the holidays. Now that it's November, the peak family-gathering season is coming. She is surely going to request that I ask for a couple of extra days off for both Thanksgiving and Christmas, since I didn't do it last year, and I haven't been home in, well, a while.

I'm not planning on going back this year, either. That small town grind, where everyone knows you and no one stays out of your business just isn't part of my lifestyle anymore. Now, it feels more like a speed bump whenever I go back home. I can't afford that now, not when I feel like I'm getting closer to Mr. Erkin–and that CEO position. Just a few more years, and I'll be set.

"You might want to take it," Gloria tells me when I hesitate to answer. There's something somber in her face that makes me take notice.

"Okay," I say, tugging on my lapels. "Send her through then." As Gloria begins to turn away, I ask, "Did she mention what it's about?"

She shakes her head and gives me a tight-lipped smile.

I nod, which is actually just me masking a strained gulp. What is this feeling in my stomach? Gloria is efficient and knows my habits well, interrupting my workflow only if it's serious. I've often had her tell my mother that I'll call her back later. So, if Gloria is insisting that I take the call….

My desk phone rings twice before I pick it up. "Mom, how are you?"

She sniffles before she answers. It's unmistakable. She's been crying. My heart sinks.

"Mom…."

"It's Nadine," she says with a tremor in her voice. "She collapsed in her studio today. She's in the hospital."

My mouth goes dry. My Aunt Ine? But she can't be—

"It seems serious, Travis." Her voice breaks, and now she's in tears, stuttering her words. She's clearly distressed.

"Where's Dad?" I ask.

"I don't know." She sighs. I think I hear the sound of an exasperated slap of her thigh. "He's still working, I think. I couldn't get ahold of him. I just got the call. I don't know… I haven't even seen…. She's just… what if she—"

"I'll be on the next flight," I tell her without thinking. "Just sit tight, and I'll be there as fast as I can."

Though I am ambitious and work hard, I try not to be a workaholic like my father. All my life, I hated seeing my mom waiting up for him at night. And while I don't have anyone waiting up for me, I don't want to create that habit for if I do one day. I strive to work more efficiently, getting the work done within reasonable hours, and I've been managing it well so far.

Then again, I haven't taken a vacation or a sick day in several years, but I call that dedication. Either way, I make sure to balance work with some leisure time at home or out with friends. And now, especially if my father isn't going to be there, and especially with my Aunt Ine in the hospital with some kind of serious ailment, I need to be there for Mom.

"Oh!" Mom exclaims. "The doctors are coming."

"Go on," I tell her. "Go talk to them. I'll be heading out shortly."

My mom exhales a shaky breath. "I love you, baby," she says, sniffling again.

I clear my throat. She hasn't called me that since I was in high school. My friends used to make fun of me for it, but it never bothered me much. Now, my heart twists for her. "I love you, too, Mom."

I wait for her to hang up, which is only a short couple of seconds later, then step out of my office. Gloria seems to be waiting for news by the way she's sitting stock straight with her hands clasped perfectly atop one another in her lap. She meets my eyes immediately.

"Can you make arrangements for my immediate departure? I'll be flying to Vermont right away," I tell her.

I take my cell phone out of my pocket, noting that the six missed calls I'd ignored, starting with the one in the elevator, were from my mother, and she has also sent me twice as many texts. She must be scared dealing with this on her own. Nadine is her big sister, her rock, her protector.

Dad is here and there, but usually preoccupied with work. He can be dependable when he needs to be. My mom has never had to deal with too many important things on her own. But I don't think he fully understands Mom's relationship with her sister. He's a good man, but dealing with others' emotions isn't exactly his strong point.

I'm scrolling through Mom's texts when Gloria puts her hand on my arm. I didn't even notice her getting up. "Travis? What about the presentation? Mr. Erkin is expecting you to—"

"I'll figure out how to do it remotely," I tell her. I squeeze her hand lightly and give her an encouraging smile.

"It's serious, then?" she asks, a couple of worry lines deepening between her brows.

"I think so, but I won't know the whole situation until I get there. But I need to go."

She nods and sits back down at her desk. "I'll text you the flight information." She gets to work right away, and I grab my coat off the hanger and shove my arms into it as I swiftly walk to the elevator.

With the morning rush over, and lunch not quite here yet, the ride down is pretty quiet. My phone dings with the flight information, and I look up at my reflection in the metal doors.

Mom always says I take after Aunt Ine. I look like her, talk like her, and love the same things she loves. Sometimes, Mom even jokes that I should have been Nadine's kid. I think that was her way of sharing me with her sister since Aunt Ine didn't have children of her own. And really, she has always felt like a second mom to me.

And now, she's in the hospital, and it's serious. My chest tightens as I try not to let my mind wonder about the unknown.

CHAPTER 3

CALLY

AUTUMN, IVY, AND I ARE HAVING A FUN DAY TOGETHER AT THE MALL IN Grant, the next town over. Honestly, I'm so happy to spend this time with them. I live alone now since I graduated from culinary school. I love my parents, but it was time for me to move out on my own like an adult, and I still see them at the cafe basically every day.

With Ivy and Autumn both so busy lately, I've had a lot of free time… alone. I'm discovering that I don't really like a solitary lifestyle, so I'm grateful to be with them now.

We walk through the mall with our pinkies hooked together, with Autumn in the middle, just like we've done since we were in grade school. Being with these two lovely people makes my heart sing. I know I can be myself with them. I know I can depend on them. And they know they can depend on me, too.

"Ooh, Cally!" Ivy exclaims, her two brown braids bouncing. "You love this store! Help me pick something out?"

"For what?" I ask, following along as she pulls Autumn and me into Punk-a-Roo's, one of my favorite clothing boutiques. This store is known for its wide array of styles, which is why I like it so much. They've got everything from cottage core, to goth, to anime girl, to sporty streetwear, so whatever I'm feeling, I have a cute outfit to express it.

Apparently, I'm known around town as one of the quirky ones. Some people might call it weird, depending on how narrow-minded they are. In high school, I did what I wanted, made splashes, rebelled at times… but I'd lost my spark after my senior year when I got voted Most Unusual along with the guy who openly picked his nose. That was a real vibe killer. But that was so long ago, almost an entire decade, and things are different now.

People don't—usually—look at me so strangely anymore. Of course, I also don't wear neon stockings and dye my hair blue anymore. I've moved past the bright colors phase. But I do enjoy dressing in funky outfits and mixing unexpected clothing items together for a whole new look. Unlike Autumn, who is just a simple, easy-going, sweater-wearing sort of girl, and Ivy, who has some kind of cozy gamine cottage core vibe, I don't really fit into a particular style. I just wear what I like.

"I don't know," Ivy sighs. She sounds a little defeated. "I think I just need to switch things up a little. I feel like I've gotten into a rut in the last couple of weeks. Help me find something to make me feel alive again!"

Autumn flicks a glance at me. Ivy is the type of girl who seems calm and reserved, sort of shy, though she can be fairly outgoing and professional around the guests at her parents' bed-and-breakfast, Hearthlight Inn. But then, when she's alone with her best buddies, she's all drama, humor, and hyperbole. Nobody would ever guess that from the amount of brown she wears.

"Well, I will be having a bridal shower at some point, right?" Autumn teases us. "Why don't we look for outfits for that?"

Ivy leans behind Autumn's head to stare at me with wide eyes. "Are we supposed to be planning that already?" she mouths.

I giggle and shrug, pursing my lips into a pout. Autumn clearly knows what's going on because she spins around and crosses her arms, looking between us like a couple of misbehaving teens.

"It doesn't have to be soon! But it's your job as my best friends and my bridesmaids!"

The three of us rummage through the store for almost two hours, spending over thirty minutes in the dressing room trying on all the clothes we pick out. I find Ivy a nice white cotton blouse, a camel sweater to wear over it, and an adorable ankle-length floral skirt that will be so cute with the boots she already has.

Autumn picks out a few things, continuing the white theme but with a different purpose. I help her choose some golden leafy hair accessories that I think suit her perfectly. And I, like usual, walk out of the store with a bag full of mismatched blouses and pants.

"What's next?" Ivy groans, seeming a little drained by the amount of time we've already spent here.

"I might like to check out the kitchen store," I say timidly, knowing that my friends are already tired and that I could easily spend another two hours in there comparing skillets and silicone utensils and reading ratings on the durability of knife sets and small appliances. I expect at least a little resistance, but I'm met with excitement instead.

"Oh, yeah!" Autumn exclaims. "I love it when you buy new kitchen stuff! It means you'll be making something delicious to share with us!"

I laugh. "Well, I've got to have someone to test it out on."

Ivy perks up. "We're not complaining! At all!"

We head into the kitchen store, our paper shopping bags bumping together. Since this is really more my territory than either of theirs, they just follow me around and ask me what this or that is for. Then we find the mother lode: the seasonal section. It has everything I need for the holiday season, particularly for Thanksgiving–Dutch ovens and pie pans, pasta makers and bakers, mashers, processors… and baking gadgets!

Now, dessert isn't necessarily my area of expertise, but it is perhaps the most fun in terms of shaping and designing. We spend half an hour at the cookie cutter wall picking the best shapes for the upcoming dinner feast. Ivy and Autumn both share in my enthusiasm, picking up things to show me and oohing and awing when I tell them how I can use each tool to make my Thanksgiving creations look extra special.

"Please, please, please invite us for Thanksgiving this year!" Ivy begs, grabbing my arm with mock desperation.

Autumn nods along. "Lukas would love it, I know."

"Friendsgiving, then?" I suggest.

Everyone is giddy with excitement at the thought, especially me. One thing about having two super cool and supportive friends is that I can share anything with them, even my new cooking creations, whenever the inspiration strikes. And they rarely fight me on it.

Exhausted from four hours of shopping, talking, and carrying our newly purchased loads, we collapse into the fast food chicken place in the food court and down three piece meals with large fries and sodas.

"I cannot do this often if I'm getting married in… well, whenever the wedding will be. I'm so bloated already." Autumn groans, patting her belly.

"You'd better get on that," Ivy tells her with a mouthful of a couple of Autumn's leftover fries. Even though Autumn is the most active and the tallest, and I am the cook of the group, Ivy can out-eat us any day of the week. "How can we plan a bridal shower if we don't even know the wedding date?"

"They'll figure it out eventually," I say. "They just got engaged a couple of weeks ago!"

"I feel like we keep talking about the wedding and the engagement," Autumn says. "I wanna hear about you guys. Cally, how about your plans, you know, with your dad and the restaurant?"

Ivy munches on her fries with her cheeks stuffed like a chipmunk and watches me expectantly. It's no secret that I'll probably take over the family restaurant one day, and I know they'll both be supportive when I do.

"My dad still resists changing any of the original recipes," I tell them. "He says that people want what they're expecting. I know it's true, but at times, it feels a little restricting. I still enjoy working there, no doubt, but I wonder sometimes…."

"That makes sense," Ivy says. "People love predictability. And your parents' place has been successful for more than a decade now. I don't blame him for sticking to his guns."

I nod. I understood too, really. "Well, even if I don't always get to share new recipes there, I'll at least have the Maple Falls Annual Fall Craft & Bake Sale Event. Man, they really need to rename that. It's a mouthful."

Every year, Maple Falls hosts a citywide bake sale and crafting event. Every food-related business, and a lot of home cooks, too, spend hours making goodies to share with the whole town. We all get to share the recipes we love. It seems the event is growing, especially over the last three years or so since Mrs. Wen won the contest with her triple-layer harvest pie. She made it into newspapers across the state.

"I can feel it!" I say with gusto, pounding my fist into the table with a sudden sense of pride. "This is my year to take Mrs. Wen down!"

Ivy stifles a laugh. Autumn raises her eyebrows and looks at me with a smirk. "Someone has to do it, eventually. It should be you."

I rest back into my plastic chair and let out a steady breath. "You know, I've never said this aloud before, but even if it doesn't happen this year or next, someday I hope one of my innovations draws national attention. It would be great for me and for the town! Maybe it will bring a bunch of new people in to experience our lovely little Maple Falls. It'll be good for you, too! Autumn, your tour guide business would get slammed in the best way! And Ivy, your family's bed-and-breakfast would—"

"Also get slammed!" she says, slapping her hand on the table. It draws a couple of worried looks in our direction, which instantly reminds her she's out in public. She retreats back into her shell and quiets down.

"It's like we're the working superhero squad of Maple Falls! We'll make sure there's a steady flood of tourists that never dries up!"

Autumn chirps, and a quiet ding from her phone pulls her attention away. "Lukas has something he wants to do tonight," she says, typing a message and then sliding her phone into her purse.

"I guess that means we should get going, then," I say regrettably.

Ivy shoves the remaining fries from all our meals into her mouth and helps me throw the trash away. Then, we haul our stuff into her SUV and head back to Maple Falls. Lukas picks Autumn up at my house, but Ivy decides to stick around with me.

"Are we going to talk about this now?" she asks.

I nod and close the door, shutting out the cool November air.

We settle at my little round dining room table with two steaming cups of hot apple cider, and I heft the three-ring binder onto the tabletop with a thud.

"I think we're well-prepared," Ivy says, opening the binder to the first tab.

The three of us have been working on our dream weddings since middle school, when we got that cute young math teacher that everyone and their grandmother had a crush on him. Every scrap of inspiration, every glittery wish, and each fondant-covered cake idea has been taped and glued into the one hundred or so pages within the sacred binder. There is a section for each of us, and to nobody's surprise, our little romance-reading girlie Autumn has the biggest one.

"Oh, yeah," I say, smoothing my hand over the handwritten notes and meticulously laced stickers. "This is going to be lit."

Ivy takes notes as we go through the book, drawing inspiration from each page of Autumn's dream wedding that she's been planning for fifteen years. I'm not sure how the book landed at my place when I was sure I'd be the last to get married.

Even semi-shy Ivy is a little love-swept more often than I am. She's at least dated since graduating from high school. I can't say the same, not really. I've been on dates, sure, but nothing ever measured up, and half the time, it was more like hanging out with a guy friend. And now, there isn't anyone else of interest left.

By the end of the night, Ivy is in dreamland with her nostalgic desires for true love. She's on her third trip through her own section, saying, "Oh, Cal, what if it's a triple wedding just like we always wanted?"

I laugh, but it's a little stifled. "You got a man that I don't know about?"

She blushes a little but shakes her head. "No, I don't suppose I do."

A quiet, deep sort of sadness settles in my chest. I guess marriage and happily ever afters are a long way off for me, too, while Autumn's is impending, and Ivy has a never-ending supply of hope for that kind of thing.

I give her a sympathetic frown. "Sorry, dear, but I don't think it's likely the three of us will get married at the same time."

CHAPTER 4

I'm in a taxi on the way into Maple Falls when I lose cell service. It's a pretty standard occurrence in this area, but I've never felt more annoyed than now. Not only am I waiting for an update from my mom about my aunt, but I'm also trying to coordinate a new meeting time with my boss to give him the presentation. I've asked Gloria to make the arrangements for me for either a video conference or to reschedule an in-person meeting for another day. With neither cell service nor an offline connection to keep perfecting my presentation, I'll also need to find time to finish it when I can get online, but my aunt is a priority right now. I'll have to figure that out later.

For now, my hands are tied, so I just sit in the backseat of the taxi and stare out the window. The world around me seems to move much slower and is full of color. It's been so long since I've made this drive or seen this view. It's eye-catching, capturing my mind and slowing the high-speed hamster wheel of worry I've been fighting for the last few hours. I let my gaze slide over the earth tone-rich world, punctuated by the vibrant colors of autumn. The landscape is dense with sycamores, maples, oaks, and birches. My favorite has always been the birch trees. I love the way the white bark contrasts against the golden senescence of the fall foliage.

I used to sit on the bank beside the Kissing Bridge with my Aunt Ine drawing the wildlife and trying to capture Maple Falls's essence with a mix of yellows, oranges, and reds. It always amazed me how she could get the colors to match perfectly in her sketchbook. Aunt Ine always chooses the right color, but she always praises my ability to sketch textures. I'm not sure how I learned to do that—it just came naturally. My fingers know how to make the little valleys and ridges of tree bark and the delicate bumps and veins of the leaves take shape.

Aunt Ine didn't teach me so much as watched me grow and gave me tips here and there. I really looked forward to summers and school breaks with her. While my parents were working, I'd be off with her. Since she was a teacher and worked at the same school I went to, we always had the same days off, and I always had a babysitter. So, we hung out together often. During the summer, I probably spent more time with her than with my parents. We hiked and explored the city for hours, and we'd stop right in the middle of the park or a random patch of wildflowers when the inspiration hit one of us to draw the scene.

The Maple Falls sign catches my eye out the window. It sits a couple of miles outside of town, denoting the narrow little asphalt highway that will lead right into the town's center. The driver slows to accommodate the drop in the speed limit, and it gives me an extra couple of seconds to admire the Maple Falls 'Welcome' sign that my aunt painted several years ago. It's a picturesque scene of the town square, lively with fall festival activities and people laughing and strolling down the street. "Maple Falls" is written in big, round orange letters outlined in creamy white with a dim shadow behind it. I always felt proud to tell people that my aunt painted that sign because everyone loved it. Everyone loves her.

God, please let her be okay, I pray silently.

For a moment, as the little houses on the outskirts of town come into view, I think about how I might sketch them. Could I match the texture of the shingles and forsythia bush in the corner of the yard? Could I capture the wave of the American flag hanging off the front porch or the wisp of branches in the trees beside it?

But I'm not certain I can even sketch anymore. I haven't even held a pencil in such a long time. The closest I've come to drawing anything is making red pen corrections on a document.

I shake my head to clear my thoughts. I should be concentrating on more important matters. I don't have time to consider textures and movement or whether I could draw scenes at all. I'm not going to be here that long, anyway. I just need to make sure that my aunt is all right, that Mom feels secure and supported, and that I get the presentation to my boss in a timely manner. Then I'll be headed back to Chicago, where my life is.

EVEN THOUGH IT'S BARELY PAST SIX O'CLOCK WHEN I ARRIVE AT MY parents' house, the evening sun is already retreating into the silky darkness, just leaving hints of soft purple and flecks of deep crimson. I haven't witnessed a sunset quite like this in some time, with so much open space. Somehow, without the light pollution, the world seems bigger in this small town. There's more to see without the bustling sidewalks and the towering buildings crowding me in.

I grab my bag and exit the taxi, thanking the driver. Gazing around, I take in the scene of my childhood neighborhood with some hesitation. Everything is the same, yet something about this place feels different. Or maybe I feel different. Regardless, the streets are quiet except for the Carlsons' old cocker spaniel, which I'm surprised is still kicking, and the faint buzz of a nearby streetlight about to flicker out. The air is still and cool, like the whole town is holding its breath.

I step onto my parents' front porch and let out a long sigh.

The porch light sconce glows a fiery yellow, and I can see the silhouette of my mother pacing back and forth in the living room. Why do I feel so nervous? I'm worried about my aunt, sure, but there's another troubling feeling lurking in my gut. I absentmindedly rub my knuckles against my chest as if I can ward this strange sensation away. Then, I put my hand on the doorknob and turn it.

My mom is just passing through the hallway, and she stops dead in her tracks and immediately breaks into tears when she sees me. Without a word, she rushes across the room and flings herself into my arms. Naturally, I drop the handle of my suitcase and embrace her.

I let her cry on my shoulder, just as I've been doing since... I can't remember how long. My mom has always been emotional, and with my dad so focused on working in his shop–and maybe being the cause of some of Mom's emotional distress–I have always been the one she leaned on for support. I glance around the room for any sign of my father, but I hadn't seen his truck in the driveway a moment ago, so I don't expect to see him. I wish he were here.

"What have the doctors told you about her?" I ask my mother.

She loosens her grasp around my waist and sighs. "They said it was a stroke. She didn't show up for work, and everyone was worried, so they called me. I went over to check on her. I don't know how long she had been like that, lying on the floor alone. If she didn't live by herself, maybe...."

Her words drift off, and I settle my hands atop my mother's shoulders and squeeze. "Don't blame yourself for anything," I tell her. "Nobody could have known this would happen."

My mom frowns but nods, accepting my answer.

"So, how is she now?" I ask, releasing her.

She wraps herself up in a hug, each hand against the opposite elbow. "She's sleeping, I guess. The doctors are waiting for her to wake up to see how much damage has been done."

I'm no medical expert, but I do remember learning that the longer a stroke goes untreated, the worse the effects are. I just hope that it's not too severe.

A long moment of silence passes between us, and I feel a little uncomfortable for some reason. This is my mother in front of me, but I haven't seen her in person in probably two years. My mind is heavy with concern for my aunt, and my chest is tight from just the thought of returning home. I guess part of me knows that Maple Falls always comes with a little bit of baggage and responsibility.

"Your room is still just like it was when you left last," she says somberly. "I don't have the heart to change my baby boy's room."

"Mom...."

I swallow down some thick, hard emotion, then grab my suitcase and follow her down the hallway to the end of the house. My room is just as she said, the same as when I left last. And when I was here two years ago, it was the same as it had been when I left after college, when I was a fresh twenty-two-year-old desperate to get out of this suffocating little town.

The bed is made, the navy quilt tucked in nicely to the full-size bed, the two-tone plaid pillowcases propped up against the wooden headboard. The nightstand is bare, save for a three-legged metal lamp and a little black alarm clock. Under the window that overlooks the street sits my desk. A gray cup holds a few sketching pencils of varying lengths, and a leather-bound sketchpad sits perfectly in the center of the desk.

"I guess I did switch out your sketches," my mother says, rubbing her finger along a black-framed landscape scene I drew in my first year of college. It's a panoramic view of Chicago's skyline, the place I dreamed of escaping to.

I let my eyes linger on the image for a little too long.

"What time are visiting hours over?" I ask finally.

My mother glances at the digital alarm clock on the nightstand. "They'll end in about two hours."

I release my bag at the foot of the bed. I'll take care of it later.

"Let's go then," I say, itching to get out of my old room, not that I will find the hospital any more comforting.

CHAPTER 5

CALLY

"OH! ARE YOU GOING TO MAKE THOSE PUMPKIN PIE BARS AGAIN!?" Autumn squeals. "I'd forfeit a month's wages for one of those."

She is sitting at the kitchen island at Maple Falls Cafe, practically drooling all over my apple twist turnovers. We're closed for the night, so it's time to go crazy baking everything I'll take to the sale tomorrow.

"Just one?" I ask over my shoulder, giving her a raised eyebrow.

She closes her eyes and takes a deep whiff, as if she can smell them before I've so much as pulled the ingredients out of the cabinet. "One whole sheet of them."

I chuckle and smooth out my patchwork apron. To put me in the right frame of mind for fall baking, I'm wearing the one that reminds me of a scarecrow. It's not the creepy, lingering-in-the-dried-up-cornfield kind, but the cutesy straw-stuffed, plaid-shirt wearing kind. It's my seasonal apron for the month of November. Inside the smaller front pocket is the timer I set for the caramel stuffed snickerdoodles.

"There's still another four minutes left," I tell myself out loud, swirling around to fetch the items for the double dark chocolate bars. Then, I check the food dehydrator for the raspberries that I'll use to top them. Something about raspberries and chocolate makes people lose their minds in the best way.

"Are you sure you don't want me to help you out somehow?" Autumn asks, sliding off the barstool with a thunk of her booties on the linoleum.

"Nah, that's okay," I say, setting up the ingredients in the order in which they'll soon be used. I gesture to the whole kitchen around us. It still smells like grease and lingering fried onions. "I'm in my element!"

Autumn smiles and cocks her head at me. "I know you've got everything under control," she says. "And maybe you're more efficient when my hands are out of it."

"And your tongue." I narrow my eyes at her and point the curved edge of a wooden spoon at her. She knows I'm referring to the time I witnessed her lick the whisk the last time I made brownies. "You know the rules! One clean spoonful!"

She rolls her eyes at me. "Yeah, yeah, kitchen warden," she grumbles. "I'm just saying that it might not kill you to have fun once in a while, too. Like, maybe stop and smell the flour."

I give her a deadpan expression. Her jokes are getting worse the more she hangs out with Lukas, though honestly, I kind of love it. "I'm a ton of fun!" I defend myself. "Ask anyone!"

"You are!" she agrees. "You're fun to be around. You're fun with clothes. You're even fun on seven hundred mile long car rides! But you, my precious little friend, are not fun in the kitchen."

I blink at her. "Just because I have an order and I like to keep things clean doesn't mean I'm not fun."

Autumn shrugs. "Okay." There is a veil of mischief in her expression telling me that she's not going to back me into a corner, nor is she going to step away from her point. Her okay is less of a white flag and more of a good-natured affront to my kitchen habits.

Her phone dings, and I know exactly who it is. "Look, your sweaty boyfriend wants to hang out with you," I say, remembering her mentioning he was playing volleyball again tonight, and sticking out my tongue.

She walks over and playfully tugs on one of the red glittery ribbons holding my hair back in pigtails. "It's fiancé now."

"Yeah, well, he's still sweaty!"

Autumn laughs out loud and shakes her head. "You're ridiculous. I love you."

I have to tease her. It's just what friends do, and we have a long history of back-and-forth jesting. It's been getting easier ever since last month when she announced her engagement. She's so caught up in everything Lukas, sometimes staring off into space thoughtfully, that she falls for my setups easier now.

I'm so happy that she found someone, and he definitely seems perfect for her. I hope I get that lucky soon.

But it's not looking very promising....

The alarm for the snickerdoodles goes off, so I pull them out of the oven and transfer them to a cooling rack.

"Well, since I can't help you make the goods, at least let me help you set them up at the bake sale tomorrow," she says. "Lukas is good at setting up tents and carrying tables. I'll even make sure he showers after his volleyball practice."

"You know I'm teasing about him being sweaty," I mumble, feeling a little guilty for picking on him when he isn't here to defend himself.

Autumn flicks my ponytail and winks at me. "I know, dearie. So, what, eight o'clock in the morning, then?"

I give her a nod. She returns it with a sweet smile, quickly nabs a hot cookie off the cooling rack, and jets out of the kitchen, sucking air between her teeth and tossing the hot cookie from hand to hand.

"Serves you right for stealing!" I yell after her, giggling. I set aside a couple of them for a goodie bag that she can have tomorrow.

By the end of the long night, I've got a huge supply of baked goods and only a few hours of sleep before I need to open my booth in the park.

❀

I slide out of bed like a limp Alfredo noodle the next morning. Single digits are not my friend when it comes to early rising on a good day. The fact that I only got three hours of sleep after getting home and doing my whole nighttime routine is just icing on the cake. The net result is fierce puffy eyes that require at least five minutes of an icy gel pack and an extra layer of concealer to make myself look halfway presentable.

It takes me roughly twenty minutes to pick an outfit that feels right for the occasion. I settle on something fall-themed: a plaid miniskirt, my nifty leggings that look like tights, and an off-the-shoulder orange sweater.

I spend another fifteen minutes tying my hair back in two high braids, then I put on a cute brown lace choker and a delicate golden double-chain necklace. Finally, I add my favorite pair of knee-high black boots and a spritz of my favorite amber and plum perfume.

Now, it's off to the races....

Autumn and Lukas beat me to the restaurant, and it's no surprise that Ivy is there too, bright, chipper, beaming and ready to help out. She's wearing the cute little beret that I gave her for her last birthday. It's so perfect for her.

In a matter of minutes, the Maple Falls Cafe delivery van is filled with trays and bags of goodies and on its way. A few minutes later, we pull into a parking spot. It seems like we're the last ones to make it to the park, as every inch of grass is covered either by tables and tents or by early shoppers.

We set up the booth on the reserved curve of the sidewalk right next to the fountain. This is prime real estate because so many people stop and sit around it, giving them plenty of time to look at my wares. And when a person stops right in front of a baked goods tent for more than two minutes, they are practically guaranteed to want to walk away with something to satisfy the craving that inevitably nags at them in the back of their mind.

When 10:30 rolls around, I'm finally feeling like a person again rather than a walking pristine zombie. Thanks to the pumpkin spice latte Ivy brought me, I'm able to appreciate the fun fall atmosphere.

Fall is the season that Maple Falls does best, and it never gets old! It's especially nice that the weather is cooperating today. It's not so cold that we need outside heaters every ten feet, but there's enough of a chill in the air that a cup of warm cider or hot cocoa and a fresh-baked treat sound alluring.

After everything is set up, and Ivy puts her interior decorator's touch on the booth with fall-colored ribbons, a stack of cute little mini pumpkins, and a vase of fall flowers, I send the others of them off to check out the competition and promise to reward them with at least one cookie for each bit of helpful information from their reconnaissance mission.

"Wanna make a trade?" Gregory Anders asks. He's calling to me from his artist's booth next door. "I'll do your caricature for one of those raspberry double-chocolate bars." He wiggles his bushy gray eyebrows at me, inducing a belly laugh from me and his wife, Mary.

She brushes a wisp of her blonde hair, which is partially white around the temples, away from her eyes while rearranging his sample photos from previous customers' sittings. "You sure you should be doing that with your sugar levels on the fritz?" she chides him.

A soft glow of pink blushes on the apples of his round cheeks, right above the trim of his beard. "Now, darlin', I've been doing well. I think a bar or two of chocolate will be okay."

Mary fingers the gray and black peppered hair curling at the base of his neck. "Sure, sugar. You sure have."

It's still early enough that not too many people are coming by, so I agree to sit and let Gregory draw me.

"Your hair grew so fast!" Elise, who is setting up her items in the next booth over, comments. She has a whole stock of handmade knitted stuffed animals: chickens, pigs, and an adorable, unmistakable iguana. The kids love her stuff. I eye the little orange crab, thinking of suggesting a trade for a couple of pumpkin bars. "It must have grown a whole foot!"

Gregory's caricatures catch someone's eye.

"Go help them," I tell him. "I've got a few things I can arrange at my booth. You can finish mine later."

"Are you sure?" he asks. "It won't be much longer."

"I'm sure," I say. "Go help your customer! We have all day!"

He pauses my drawing and switches to a young high school couple who look adorable together. She's wearing a fall-themed sweater and a cute pumpkin-colored skirt that matches his shirt.

I head back to my booth, rearranging the sweet goodies and taking a sip of my latte. I look around the park and take a deep breath, taking in the beautiful scene. The sun is sending soft beams of light through the thinning trees. A couple of squirrels chase each other through the shrubs. People are filtering into the park, and many of them are gathering in groups, welcoming each other with smiles and hugs.

Almost every face is familiar to me. Even if I don't know their names, I recognize them. That's one of the best things about Maple Falls. Everyone is familiar and friendly, and they all seem happy to be here, and that makes me happy in turn.

When Gregory is finished with the young couple's sketch, he urges them to check out my booth.

"Oh, this all looks so delicious!" the girl squeals.

"Pick out anything you want," the boy tells her.

She takes a moment to look over my huge selection! She finally goes for the double-chocolate bar, and after he pays me, she feeds him the first bite. It's way too cute, and that tender act sends a bittersweet sensation through my chest.

CHAPTER 6

Travis

THE SUN SHINES BRIGHTLY, BUT ITS HEAT IS INEFFECTIVE. IT CAN'T pierce the thick layer of cold that we're trapped under. Like Chicago, Vermont can be cold as the seasons change, and now that October has passed, the chill has settled in. I shove my hands in my jacket pockets and step off the front porch of my parents' house. Immediately, I feel a fraction of the weight on my shoulders release.

It was a rough night. My aunt looked so shrunken and small lying in the hospital bed. The constant beeping of her heart monitor was eerie in the otherwise silent room. While we were there for nearly two hours, Aunt Ine didn't do more than open her eyes a few times. I can't forget the far-off, dreary look in them. She seemed so distant, like the woman I know wasn't even there.

Apparently, on top of suffering from a brain injury from the stroke, she also fell down the stairs when she lost consciousness, injuring her hip. According to the nurse, who was flitting in and out of my aunt's room last night, the doctor is keeping her pretty sedated because of the pain, and they will have to keep monitoring her condition before they can do anything about the hip injury.

I can almost hear Aunt Ine now, talking about how breaking her hip is a sign of old age and that she just won't have it. A wry smile creeps onto my face, thinking about her spunk, but it fades quickly. This is so unfair. She has always been perfectly healthy and active. Nothing like this should have happened to a person like her.

Then again, it has been some time since I've seen her in person, and our video calls have been much less frequent these last several months. I suppose I might not have noticed the signs of aging.

Guilt churns in my belly. If I were still living here in Maple Falls, would things have been different? Would I have been able to help in some way?

I hear the front door creak open behind me, but I don't want to turn around and see my mother's pained expression. "Where are you going?" she calls after me.

I'm already halfway across the yard with no intention of going back inside. I have a few things to get sorted if I'm going to be here for a couple of days, starting with my presentation. I'd been getting texts and emails throughout the evening from Gloria and my boss trying to figure out a good time for this meeting. Honestly, though, thinking about work right now, with everything my aunt is going through, makes my stomach churn even more, like a washing machine full of slush.

Before I knew the extent of my aunt's prognosis, I thought I'd be here for a couple of days and then be headed back. But now I've seen her in person, and I've spoken to the doctors. They still can't be sure about her chances of recovery until it's safe to get her off the anesthesia. Then, they'll be able to assess her motor skills and verbal function, and they'll know if she's healthy enough for hip surgery. So I'm not sure how long I'll be here now. It might be a week—maybe more.

I should probably get this presentation over with so I can focus on my aunt and my family for as long as I need to, but on the other hand, I want to be thorough so I don't miss anything important. I'm sure it could get me the promotion I want, a step up on the ladder of success in the direction that I want to go. Putting it off for too long might mean losing focus and blowing my chance at an impressive presentation.

My mind goes back to my aunt. She could literally be on her deathbed, and I'm worried about a promotion? How selfish am I?

"I'm going to run a couple of errands and then go see Aunt Nadine," I call over my shoulder.

I can almost feel my mother's eyes glaring into my back. Does she feel betrayed by me for leaving her right now? Dad has already left for the day, so she will be alone for a while now, until I get back.

I shrug off the lurking guilt that hides in the shadows of my childhood home and walk down the street. First things first. I need a rental car.

Line-Up Auto Center is just on the other side of the square, probably about a mile from home. I'll have to walk through half the town to get there, but honestly, a walk sounds nice. I'm adjusting to the cool air now, or maybe the sun is doing a better job heating things up than I thought, and I finally feel its warm rays settle on my face. I close my eyes and breathe in the fresh air. There's a faint scent of something sweet on the wind and the hint of wood smoke.

I'm only a few blocks away from my parents' house when a passing car slows. The glare of the sun on the windshield obscures the driver's face, but he definitely looks familiar. I stop in my tracks when I sense the person is looking at me, too. Soon the blue Mazda stops next to me and the window rolls down.

"Travis? Is that you?" I recognize the voice instantly, and my chest lightens.

Jeremiah Davies.

I hear him shift into park, and the door flies open. Around the fender jogs my best friend from high school. He looks the same save for a little more muscle in his shoulders and his hair styled in short dreads.

"What the heck, man? I thought you were outta here and never coming back!" he says with a wide, dimpled smile. He clasps my right hand in a firm shake and reaches the other arm around me in a bro-hug.

A soft chuckle escapes me. I really wasn't expecting to run into anyone I was close to. It's been so long since I've even spoken to Jeremiah. "Yeah, I'm just here for a little bit. How are things going?"

He juts a finger back at the car. "They're pretty dang good," he says as the passenger window rolls down. Jeremiah beams at the woman sitting there.

"Casey!" I say excitedly, letting go of my buddy and jogging over to the window. "Casey Walsh, how the heck are you?"

"It's Casey Davies now," she says, sticking her hand out the open window and showcasing a bright smile and an equally gleaming silver and diamond ring. I take her hand lightly. "He finally caught me, I guess."

She did not look displeased to be caught by Maple Falls' 400-meter State Championship gold medal winner. "That's—wow, that's so great," I say, leaning over to get a closer look. That's when I catch sight of the bump of her belly. "And you're—"

I hear the rustle of footsteps behind me, and Jeremiah claps me on the back. "You missed a lot these last couple of years," he says. His tone is warm and friendly, yet it brings back that nasty churning in my intestines. How much have I missed being away and focused on nothing but work?

"Yeah." I laugh with equal parts regret and disbelief. My best friend from high school got married, and I didn't even know it. "It looks that way."

I stand by the car and gaze back and forth between the two of them. Everyone knew these two would end up together, but Casey wanted to go off to college on her softball scholarship and didn't want to make any commitments beyond that. Last I knew, she had graduated with a nursing degree and a couple of NAIA trophies, and Jeremiah was coaching track at Maple Falls High and teaching history. I wonder how long they've been together now.

"Congratulations on the marriage and on the baby!" I tell them. "I'm... sorry I missed the wedding."

"Hey, let's get together before you leave, yeah?" Jeremiah suggests, clapping a hand on my back.

I nod. "Yeah. I'd like that."

"Babe," Casey calls, training her cornflower blue eyes on her husband. "We've gotta go. We're going to be late for the ultrasound appointment."

Jeremiah flashes another huge grin and wiggles his eyebrows. "Duty calls! We're about to find out if we're having a Cooper or a Gracie."

His smile is contagious. It's awesome to see my best friend from high school so excited to be a dad. "Hey, let me know when you're ready to paint the nursery, and I'll be there," I say with a wink. The words are out of my mouth before I process what I'm saying. Unless they're planning on painting the nursery this week, I probably won't even be around.

Jeremiah's smile falters a little, but he doesn't let it slip away completely. "Sure, buddy. It was good seeing you. I'll catch you later for that dinner, got it?"

I nod and watch my friend get in his car, kiss his wife on the cheek, then drive away. An uncomfortable sensation washes over me, but I can't quite place it, so I keep on walking down the street.

A few blocks later, I'm encroaching on the perimeter of the park. Tents sprawl along the winding pathway, and a couple of food trucks are parked alongside the street. That explains the sweet fragrance from earlier. It's some kind of festival.

Ah! It must be the annual Fall Colors Baked Goods and Craft Fair. I should have known. Maple Falls has so many festivals and events between Halloween and New Year's Eve, it seems like there is always something going on every week.

I decide to stroll through the park in case there's anything I might like to get for my aunt when she wakes up. She's always loved these events, and she has a pretty strong sweet tooth.

About five booths in, I see a sign for homemade baked goods. Something sweet always improves Aunt Ine's mood, so that seems like the best option. The booth is decorated nicely, with a few stacked pumpkins and a vase of my mom's favorite flowers—zinnias with a few sprigs of baby's breath. Trays of baked goods and packages of cookies, as well as a couple of cake stands with delicious-looking pies, fill the air with enticing aromas.

Perfect.

As I approach the tent, the woman there stands to greet me. When I look into her eyes, my chest constricts. I gulp absentmindedly, caught off guard by her wide smile and long eyelashes. Her dark hair is tied back in two long braids. She looks to be about my age, but I can't place her. All I can think is, holy heavens, she's beautiful.

"Welcome," she says, her blue eyes shining. Her voice is like a crisp fall apple, rich and sweet. She extends her hand toward me.

"Hi." I say, noticing her hand is warm despite the chill in the air.

"Long time no see, Travis." She grins at me, and when she lets go of my hand, I want to snatch hers back again.

She knows me? Wait, do I know her?

I study her face. Bright blue eyes, high cheekbones, a contagious smile…. She does look familiar.

"You're back in town?" she asks.

I realize I'm just staring at her and still slowly shaking her hand. I clear my throat and shove my hands into the pockets of my jeans. "Um, yeah, just for a little while, though."

"Well, it's nice to see you," she says. Her smile is genuine and sweet. She has a small gap between her two front teeth, almost unnoticeable, but it's… cute and endearing. "Are you interested in a sweet treat?" she asks.

It's like I've never had a thought before. My mind is totally blank. I'm in awe of this bright, beautiful woman standing in front of me. I blink twice, three times, trying to ground myself back into my surroundings.

What in the world is wrong with me?

She clasps her hands behind her back and looks up at me with a teasing smile. She definitely just caught me staring at her. I clear my throat again and force my eyes down toward the goods on the table. I hear her stifle a giggle, and a weightless sensation settles in my chest.

It's kind of like one of those moments in football when I was getting sacked and the lineman had me on their shoulder in the air, right before he slammed me on the ground.

It's kind of a rush, kind of dangerous.

If only I could remember who she is.

CHAPTER 7

I'M NOT AN AWKWARD HIGH SCHOOLER ANYMORE. I KNOW WHEN A GUY is giving me a 'wow, you're beautiful' kind of look. I just never thought I'd see that look on Travis Thatcher's face—at least not directed at me.

We were on opposite sides of the world in high school, so there never would have been a reason for him to notice me back then. Travis was the cool guy, the outgoing jock, friends with all the popular kids. He was always busy with extracurriculars and sports, and when he wasn't doing that, he had his nose buried in a textbook so he could earn the best grades and get into a good college. He was a couple of grades ahead of me, and teachers were always singing his praises by the time I sat in their classes. He even ended up graduating a semester early and going to school in Chicago—far away from Maple Falls.

Meanwhile, I was just an average girl—or maybe slightly below average to most. I had a small group of friends, and outside of them, I mostly kept to myself. The highlights of my high school career were that I participated in Family, Career, and Community Leaders of America, got second place in an art show, and graduated in the top ten percent of my class.

A lot of the other kids used to call me strange because I've always liked dressing up and wearing clothes slightly out of the norm. I wasn't necessarily bullied or anything, but I often caught people's lingering gazes. I still do once in a while, but I'm grown up, and the townsfolk are generally more open-minded. I get along with everyone, but there are certainly times when I still feel a little out of place, like nobody really sees me.

So now, while former quarterback Travis Thatcher is looking at me with a moon-eyed expression, I can't help but feel a little giddy. I always thought he was cute, but there's something about him now, an air of sophistication and maturity that's really attractive. It's been nearly ten years since he graduated from high school and moved away from town. Who knows what kind of life he's leading now?

He's looking over my baked goods on the table, but his eyes keep flicking back to me like he can't help himself. I study him, feeling a swarm of cicadas circling in my chest. This is exciting, being under his gaze. It's like he's intrigued, but he doesn't know what to do about it. And I don't think he remembers me.

When his eyes settle on me again, I catch them purposefully. "Do you see something you like?" I ask with a coy smile, holding his gaze. My bravado wins me a shocked smile from him, like he knows he's been caught staring.

His grin widens, and he slides a hand through his ruffly blond hair. "Everything looks great," he says, maintaining eye contact like I've prompted a flirty challenge, his full confidence returned. "Did you make this all yourself?"

My face freezes in a permanent smile. Wait, is he flirting with me? I kind of hope so.

I hold up my hands and wiggle my fingers. "These two hands and about five hours in the kitchen," I tell him.

Travis gives a little laugh. "No helpers?"

I shake my head. "My friends are better at eating than they are at baking, though I have to give them credit for helping me get this tent set up this morning."

"You have your own bakery or something?" he asks, sounding genuinely interested.

I'm flattered. I want to tell him that I do, that I have my own super successful, super impressive store. Too bad I can't say that, not yet. "Not exactly," I confess. I point down the street. "I'm still working for my parents at the Maple Falls Cafe."

His eyes brighten with something like recognition. "Yeah? Right, I love that place. So if I stop by for a classic burger sometime soon, you'll be there?"

Wait what? My heart stops. My arms tingle. Is he planning on seeking me out!?

I manage a nonchalant nod, and then I add, "If you wait long enough, you might even witness me take over the restaurant."

"Really?" Travis asks. "Owning a restaurant is hard business. You must be ambitious."

Is it the compliments he's giving me or the enchantment of his beautiful, rich, olive green eyes that has my head swirling? Whatever it is, my confidence is peaking. "You'll have to stick around for one of my specials. It'll be on the menu soon," I tell him.

Travis leans toward me a little, his smile deepening. "I like the sound of that."

I can feel my neck heating up. Just what is going on with me? I've never felt so… flirty before. "Until then, you can get a taste with one of these." I gesture at the table.

"I'll take the bait," he laughs. "What do you recommend?"

Am I on fire? It's a cool autumn day, but I swear I'm standing on the sun.

But wait, a guy like him probably has a girlfriend….

"I guess that depends on who it's for," I respond, crossing my arms beneath my chest.

His smile weakens a bit, but it's still bright. Am I being too obvious? Does he see through my question? "My Aunt Nadine, actually."

He rests his hand on the sewn-together lace doily tablecloth, tapping his finger lightly.

I ease up a little, sensing a change in his demeanor. "All right then," I say, surveying my goodies. He's so close, only a couple of feet away, still watching me intently. "I guess the next thing to consider is the reason for the gift."

Glancing up at him, I watch the rest of his charming smile fade. His green eyes turn mossy. "She's, uh, in the hospital right now. I just want to get her something she can enjoy when she wakes up."

My heart aches for him, and I want to put a hand on his arm, but I don't really know him, so I plant my hand over my heart instead. "Oh, my gosh, I'm so sorry to hear that," I say. "I always loved Ms. Endicott. She was my favorite teacher in elementary school. She's still teaching, right? Or…?"

Travis arches an eyebrow as he watches my reaction and gauges a response. "Yeah, she is, or was, I guess. The doctors aren't really sure yet how much the stroke affected her.

"What? A stroke! That's… that's terrible." My heart drops into my stomach. "I'm so sorry." This conversation has suddenly taken a sour turn. I search his face for some sign of what to say or do next.

"I appreciate that," he finally says after a brief silence. "She, uh, really likes chocolate and cinnamon."

I give him a reassuring smile and take a step around the table. I pick up a package of caramel snickerdoodles and a double-chocolate raspberry bar. "Here. I think she'll love these, then. And please tell her hello for me when she wakes up."

His expression lightens a little bit more, which in turn eases the clinching in my chest. He must be going through a lot. I suppose that's why he's back in town. He seems so concerned for his aunt, though, understandably. I'm almost sorry that I was flirting with him just seconds ago.

"Sure. I'll do that. How much do I owe—" He's reaching into his jacket pocket for his billfold, but I put my hand out to stop him.

"Nothing." I shake my head.

He turns his head slightly, his eyes wide. "I couldn't possibly just take these. You're here to make a profit, right? So let me—"

I wave him off. "I'm here to share some sweet, delicious treats with whomever wants to try some. I'm really not worried about a few dollars. She has always been so good to me. Please, just take them for her. I insist."

Travis gives me an easy, lopsided smile that tips up on the left side. "Then," he begins, pointing to the apple pumpkin-shaped pastries, "let me buy one of those for myself."

I grin and nod. While I'm placing one in a small paper bag, I see him slip a ten in my tip jar, so I give him another. It's really been a good day. I've probably made a sizable profit from this event already, and there are still a few more hours, so I could afford to extend my appreciation in this small way.

He takes the bag and places the treats for his aunt inside as well. I think he's about to turn and leave as it seems like our interaction has reached a natural stopping point, but he just stands there looking at me. Again. It's a little different from the first time, less awe and more intent. It makes my cheeks flush, and for once, I'm grateful that my already ruddy cheeks from the cool air can hide my blush.

"So, um, please tell Ms. Endicott that I hope she enjoys the treats and gets better soon," I say, not exactly wanting to urge him on, but also feeling the need to fill the silence.

Just as Travis is opening his mouth to respond to me, there's a shrill shriek nearby. "No way! Travis?"

As I spin around to find the source of the sound. A blur of dark hair whooshes past, nearly knocking me into my table. Travis shields the goodies in his bag but catches the body flying into his arms with a bewildered look on his face. He cranes his neck back to see who has literally thrown herself at him, and a little smile creeps back onto his face.

"Luann," he says, surprised. "Wow."

Wow? My chest tightens with jealousy, and I hate myself for it. Of course it's Luann Britzen, the captain of the cheerleading squad from high school. I remember they hung out a lot in high school. All the star athletes spent time with the cheerleaders. Travis and Luann probably dated then.

I can't help but watch their interaction unfold in front of me, but I feel like I'm suddenly pushed into the background even though I'm standing just a few feet away. I'm the side character in their movie, the eccentric art nerd always hovering in the corners.

Travis eases Luann back a few inches but keeps an arm around her shoulders. They must be comfortable together, even after all these years. Maybe they kept in touch or something.

"Oh, my goodness! It's been too long! What have you been up to?" she gushes loudly.

Travis smiles in an awkward, but charming, way, as if he didn't expect to be greeted like he's a celebrity. "Just working mostly," he says. He finally drops his arm from around her.

"What are you doing here now, though, and without warning like this?" Luann bats him on the arm playfully.

He just gives a small shrug. "I wasn't expecting to come here either. I'm actually on the way to the hospital—"

"What?! Oh, my gosh! No way! What happened?"

I barely catch Travis looking over Luann's head back in my direction. I force a little smile and tilt my head in a weird sort of good-bye bow. I turn and walk back under my tent, sinking down in the chair behind the setup of tables.

Rather than get involved in their reunion, I look in the opposite direction where a little girl who's about eight is getting her caricature drawn.

I hear Travis briefly tell Luann about his aunt, and the next time I glance in that direction, they're walking away. Luann is practically glued to his hip. I bet the two of them will be strolling along hand-in-hand in a few moments.

I roll my eyes at myself for thinking that he could ever possibly have been interested in me. I was hoping to maybe get to know him again after all of this time.

But oh, well! I guess it's just not meant to be.

CHAPTER 8

Travis

Before I know it, Luann is leading me across the park, past all the colorful tents, and going on about how she's so happy to see me.

"Really, Trav," she continues. "I'm so sad we've lost touch these last couple of years. I always looked forward to your coming back to town, but then you just disappeared."

I laugh stiffly. I didn't want to come back, and I certainly didn't want to come back under these circumstances. It's not like I planned on running into anyone I used to know, but Jeremiah and Luann were two of my best friends in high school, so I'm glad I did. Running into Jeremiah was great. It looks like he's doing well with Casey and the baby on the way. But Luann....

"I'm just so sad about your aunt, though," she continues. "It sucks that this has to be the reason we're reunited." She wraps her arm around mine and squeezes just a bit too tightly.

"Yeah," I respond blankly, not exactly hiding my irritation—not that she's noticed. She interrupted my conversation with that woman... whose name is on the tip of my tongue. She mentioned her parents' restaurant, Maple Falls Café. But I just can't remember the name of the quirky girl who waited tables there and hung out in the kitchen.

Luann walks me the rest of the way to the Line-Up Auto Center, where I'll pick up my rental car. "So, how long do you think you'll be in town?" she asks, peering up at me.

I pull my arm out of her grasp. "I'm not sure yet. Aunt Ine didn't look very well last night. I want to make sure she's doing okay before I leave."

"You are such a good man, Trav." Luann bats her eyelids at me.

I shrug. I'm here because of the severity of my aunt's condition. I haven't spoken to or called her in a few months, and I even avoid talking to my own parents most of the time. Heck, I was just flirting with that girl at the baked goods tent even though I'm on the way to see my still-unconscious aunt. And that presentation is still lingering in the back of my mind. I'm not sure the phrase "good man" fits me at the moment.

Line-Up Auto is decorated in a sports theme, mostly football and baseball. I recognize the man behind the counter, not just because he's been working here my whole life, but because I saw him at every single one of my games in high school. Harold is a sports enthusiast, to say the least. He can name every Super Bowl and World Series winner since the beginning of time, and he has the stats about every high school game memorized since he was in elementary school— winners, losers, scores, everything.

Luann follows me in as I greet him, and we shake hands.

"I've got the best vehicle for you, hall-of-famer," Harold tells me.

I laugh awkwardly. He's the only one who has ever called me that. Apparently, he had high hopes for me back in high school. But I declined any offers to play college football, to many people's dismay. At the time, I just wanted to focus on getting a good job and gaining some independence. I had my heart set on Chicago, and none of the colleges there were interested. My biggest concern at the time had been getting out of Maple Falls and leaving it all behind.

Luann is still tailing me when I find the navy-blue Challenger in a row of cars, between a minivan and a little white sedan.

"Can I come with you to the hospital?" she asks. "I'd love to see Ms. Endicott." She smiles brightly, lingering by the driver's side door.

"I don't think so," I say as gently as I can. "This is a private family matter right now. Maybe you can plan a visit after we find out how she's really doing."

She twirls a strand of her hair the way she's always done whenever she's disappointed, but she nods anyway. "Sure. I understand."

I tell her goodbye and start to get in the car, but she takes a step toward me. "Wait, Travis," she says. "Let me give you my number, so you can let me know when it's a good time to see her or… to see you." A coy smile slides into place on her face.

Luann has always been the kind of girl who gets what she wants. She's confident in her ability to flirt to get anything she wants. I'd like to give her the benefit of the doubt since we're older now, and surely we've both changed, but the way she's batting her eyelids at me makes me wonder how sincere she is. We were good friends back then, and she did have a good relationship with my aunt throughout high school.

"That's fine," I tell her, turning around. "I'm sure she'll be happy to know she'll have a visitor when she's feeling up for it."

I give Luann my phone so she can put her number in it. When she hands it back, I notice she's added a little swirling star emoji by her name.

"Promise you'll text me or call me?" she purrs as I climb into the car.

I nod in silent agreement and shut the door. I offer a short wave as I crank the engine and shift into gear. I'm glad to see her in the rearview mirror as I pull away.

As I'm passing by the park again, I see the rows of tents still lined up, and my mind goes back to Cally. Cally! That's her name! I squeeze the steering wheel and smile to myself. Of course… Cally.

I try to spot her tent, but everything just blurs together. The bag of treats is on the passenger seat where I tossed it, so I wrestle one-handed to fish a pastry out, laughing out loud when I realize she has given me two. I pop half of one in my mouth. The crust is perfectly flaky, and the creamy apple filling is sweet. There's a little extra spice in there that I can't place, and it enhances the pastry's flavor.

Dang, that's good. I stuff the other half of the pastry in my mouth just as I'm passing the Maple Falls Café.

Man, the pieces are coming together now. I remember seeing Cally more at the café than at school. She must have been a grade or two below me. I did notice her around campus occasionally, but she was a lot different then. She had this sort of quirky nerd vibe back then. She always dyed her hair and wore bright colors. I guess we didn't really have that much in common.

But now, that is certainly not the case. She's confident—and strikingly beautiful. Her hair must be back to its natural color now, jet black, and the color looks incredible with those striking blue eyes. Plus, she seems excited to take over her family's restaurant one day. I was instantly intrigued, even before I remembered her name. I wanted to talk to her more—but then Luann showed up….

I shake my head. Here I go again, thinking about something else when my aunt is still in the hospital, and we aren't even sure she'll recover.

My phone chimes, jerking me out of those thoughts. My mom's name flashes across the screen, and I'm grateful. I need to focus on the true issue at hand. I answer and put her on speaker. "Mom. Any news?"

"Travis. They've taken your aunt off the sedation drugs. She's starting to wake up a little. Where are you? I thought you were going to be here by now," my mother's voice comes through half-scolding, and I realize she's driven herself to the hospital. I thought she was going later.

"I just got my rental car, Mom," I explain. "I'll be there soon. I'm just a couple of miles away."

She huffs into the phone, and I recognize that tone.

"Is Dad there?" I ask, even though I know it can be a touchy question.

The line is quiet except for a light rustling in the background. "Just get here soon, please. Your aunt will be delighted to see you."

When I finally make it to the hospital, I stop outside my aunt's room. She's lying down, but her bed has been inclined slightly, and she's looking around the room with groggy eyes. She's still attached to the oxygen and heart monitor, and she has an IV in her arm. My mom sits in a chair pulled up close to her bed, clasping her sister's hand, facing away from me, so I'm sure she doesn't know I'm here yet.

"She's still coming out of it," my father says behind me.

I turn to face him, surprised. I honestly wasn't expecting him to be here, but I'm glad he is. I only saw him for a few minutes last night before bed.

"Oh, Dad," I mutter. "You made it."

He gives me a tired smile. "I've been here for a couple of hours."

That surprises me, but I just nod. "So, what's the news?" I ask instead of probing deeper into why he's taking the time away from work, which is out of character.

My father clasps my shoulder and urges me into the room. "She's doing okay. Why don't you just go in and talk to her before they take her back for the hip surgery?"

I feel like a child again, visiting my sick grandma in the hospital after her stroke. But she was much older at the time than my aunt is now, and… she didn't recover. I ignore the nauseated feeling rising in my stomach and go to Aunt Ine's bedside.

Her hazy eyes linger on me before the faintest hint of recognition appears on her face. "Tra-visss," she cries.

I crouch down closer to her, and she tries to raise her right hand to me, but it barely moves. She groans, but her smile doesn't disappear.

"Hey, Aunt Ine," I whisper, taking her cool fingers in my hand. "I came to see how you're doing."

She blinks slowly. "Good," she says. I can just make out the word. I don't know if she means that she's good or if it's good that I came to see her.

I give her a smile and look over at my mom, who is refusing to make eye contact, as she always does when she's irritated with me.

I sit down, and we make a bit of small talk, Aunt Ine smiling at me, but it's awkward, and clearly, she's struggling.

A short time later, the doctor comes in and updates us on her condition. It's obvious that the stroke has caused her to lose some functionality in her right arm—her drawing hand—as well as her right leg. She's groggy from the sedation, so they still want to monitor her speech and verbal processing, but they've deemed her healthy enough to go in for the hip repair.

The team is coming to get her in a few minutes to prepare her for the surgery, so we have just a few more moments to sit with her. The staff gives us some space. My father stands off in the corner of the room, and my mom sits in the chair on my aunt's left side. Sitting has me antsy, so I stand, rocking back and forth slightly as I keep the smile forced on my face.

"In case you need some motivation to get better faster," I say to my aunt with a light teasing tone, "I brought you some delicious treats. Since you're going in for surgery, I'll keep them fresh for you for later."

I hold up the bag so she can get a whiff of them. The plastic wrapping is a little crinkled, but the cookies look good. The chocolate bar, on the other hand, is broken in half, probably from when Luann practically tackled me. Aunt Ine's eyes brighten a little bit, and she coughs. "Thank... you."

Not long afterward, the orderlies come to take my aunt to surgery, leaving me and my parents in the quiet hospital room by ourselves. My dad doesn't make it long before he says he is going to go back to work, leaving me alone with my stressed-out, irritated mother.

It's going to be a long night of waiting.

CHAPTER 9

Cally

THE SUN IS SINKING LOWER IN THE SKY, AND IT'S TIME TO PACK UP MY tent. As promised, Autumn and Lukas stop by at five o'clock to help me tear down.

"Wow, girlie! It looks like you cleaned house today!" Autumn says cheerfully when they arrive.

It's true. I've sold nearly everything. Just a few packages of tri-flavor cookies and a few slices of various pies remain. I take note of the bestsellers so I can adjust my menu for maximum success next year.

"I sure did!" I sweep my arms and twirl in a circle under the tent. "Nobody can resist my goodies!"

Lukas chuckles and shakes his head but comes under the tent to start packing things into boxes. "We get some of the leftovers, right?" I hear him mutter to Autumn. She pinches his cheeks, literally. I've never seen her act so cutesy before. It suits her though, this whole love thing.

"I'll see what I can do." She plants a gentle kiss on his jaw.

"Right on," he says with a pump of his fist.

"You know I can hear you guys," I say flatly. "I'm literally standing three feet away."

Autumn and Lukas share an unapologetic glance. "I call dibs on the cookies," Autumn says.

A minute later, Ivy comes trotting up to us, her face flushed from either running or the cold air. "Sorry I'm late, everybody."

I cock my head and pluck something out of her hair. "Is this sawdust?"

She laughs bashfully. "I've been working on something. But I'm here now!"

I narrow my eyes at her but let it go for now. Autumn, Ivy, and I work together, first setting aside the leftover treats and then boxing up the little bits of decor that Ivy set up for me this morning. We get everything put away in less than ten minutes, leaving the tables and tents for the event committee to pick up later.

Just as we're walking away, someone calls out to me. "Thanks for being a great neighbor today!" It's Gregory. He and his wife are filing away the back stock of his paintings.

I smile, wave, and move on with my friends. It was a nice day. My treats sold well, and I enjoyed talking with Gregory and his wife. The caricature he drew of me looks like a cartoon K-pop idol, with my black hair in braids and my cat-eye makeup. It's cute and colorful, and it's so interesting to find out how other people see me. I used to be a little afraid of what people thought of me, but I think I've gained enough confidence now that it generally doesn't get to me when I catch people staring.

Except for Travis—he made me feel a little squirmy today. His gaze was so intense, like nothing could escape his attention. Maybe that sort of watchfulness has dredged up some of those old insecurities, like I was just a little afraid he might look too deeply and see something he didn't like.

Or maybe I'm reading too much into it. Since I don't even know if I'll even see him again, I shouldn't ponder this matter for too long.

Once his aunt is released from the hospital, he'll probably be itching to go back to whatever life he has found outside of Maple Falls.

But his aunt will still be around, and I am a big fan of hers. She might not remember me, but I've attended her sip and sketch classes at the library on a couple of occasions. Ms. Nadine has such a warm personality. I hope she makes a full recover.

Later, when we're making our way to my parents' restaurant for dinner, Ivy says, "You're being quieter than usual."

"Huh?" I didn't realize I was acting differently, but I suppose my mind has been lingering on earlier events. "I guess I'm just distracted."

Autumn stops dead in her tracks, causing Lukas to bump into her. She pats his chest in apology before turning fully to me and catching my wrist in her hand. "Why, what happened?"

What Travis said earlier about his aunt has stuck with me. It seems like her condition is pretty serious. Ms. Endicott was my favorite teacher in elementary school, and she's a cool person in general. After all these years working as an elementary art teacher, I'm sure she's forgotten all about me, but I remember her, and it makes me so sad to think that she's sick.

"Do you remember Ms. Nadine Endicott?" I ask.

Autumn and Ivy nod. Ivy adds, "Oh, yeah, everyone's favorite art teacher! She always took special care of you back then, posting your artwork out in the halls." She crosses her arms thoughtfully and adds, "She could never tell the difference between my horses and my dogs, but my drawings still ended up on the wall."

I smiled softly at the memory, but it feels bittersweet now. "Well, I heard today that she had a stroke and is in the hospital. It might be serious."

Autumn looks at Lukas then turns back to me. "Oh, that's awful."

"I was just thinking of doing something for her," I say. "Maybe I'll order some flowers to be delivered to her room."

Ivy nods thoughtfully. "Yeah, I want to do that, too!"

Autumn nods in solidarity. She feels her slacks and seems to notice she has no pockets. "Honey, where's my phone?" she asks

Lukas. He fishes her phone out of his jacket pocket and hands it to her, and she types something and puts the phone to her ear.

We continue walking across the street until we get to the café. Ivy and I go in to nab a table while Autumn and Lukas stand outside to finish her call. I presume she's ordering flowers for Ms. Nadine.

Sitting side by side in our usual booth, Ivy and I pull up the website for the It's Always Sunny Flower Shop. We look through the options and pick a couple to have sent to our sweet teacher.

It makes my heart feel light and warm to imagine her room filled with color and the fragrance of fresh flowers. She has done so much for others. It's time to give some of that love back.

"Hey," I say, a brilliant idea popping into my head.

Autumn slides into our booth, and Lukas climbs in behind her. They sit so close they're literally shoulder to shoulder with an entire foot of space on either side of them. It's adorable in a slightly ridiculous kind of way. I wonder what it's like to not be able to get enough of another person. I spend so much time alone lately, the idea feels foreign.

"What's up?" Autumn asks.

"I was just thinking how nice it would be to flood Ms. Nadine's room with flowers," I suggest. "We should tell everyone who loved her as much as us—"

Ivy cuts in. "And let's face it, that's probably half the town."

"Exactly," I say. "We should post that we're sending her flowers. Maybe they'll send some, too, and her whole room will be like a garden."

Autumn lets out a giddy giggle. "That would be awesome! I'd certainly feel loved and cared for if I were in the hospital with that many flowers."

"And I'm sure Mr. Johnson would appreciate the business at his flower shop," Lukas adds with a grin.

We all busy ourselves with our phones, reaching out on social media, and searching for people who might be willing to send get-well flowers and baskets to the hospital. We continue the effort over dinner.

By seven o'clock, the café is so busy, my mom is telling people they'll have to wait thirty minutes to be seated.

"I feel like I should help out," I mention, watching her hustle to keep up. Jarred is probably only two hours into his shift, but he already looks exhausted. I know our other waitress, Tamara, is due to be leaving soon. Mom will pitch in where she can, but Dad must be swamped back in the kitchen as well.

"The guilt consumes her," Ivy says in a spooky ghost voice.

I roll my eyes and knock my shoulder playfully against her. "I've got to keep up the title of Most Favorite Child."

My siblings don't care much for the family restaurant. I was always the only one hanging out with Dad in the kitchen—at home and here. They're far away now, with their spouses, growing families, and chasing their dreams of traveling and working. But this place will always be important to me.

"All right, dearie," Autumn says, clasping my hand on the table. "We'll get out of here so you can get to work. But don't forget that we need to meet soon to talk about top secret wedding stuff."

Lukas pinches his eyebrows together comically. "Secret even from me? I'm half of the wedding!"

Autumn scrunches her nose. "Some things are supposed to be a surprise, even for you. Don't worry. You'll still be in the know for ninety percent of it."

I know that the last ten percent is about her dress, and she's been racking her brain trying to come up with a special gift idea for him.

"Of course," I say with a nod. "Operation Ten Percent is underway!" That gets a laugh out of everyone.

We pay the bill, and then my friends leave, so I make my way into the kitchen. My dad wears the headband that keeps most of the sweat out of his eyes, but his shirt is damp, and beads of perspiration dot the back of his neck below his salt and pepper hair.

"Sous chef ready and waiting for orders," I say as I tie my patchwork apron around my waist.

He rarely asks for help, but I can tell he's relieved to see me join him in the kitchen.

"Rush hour snuck up on me," he says, turning his attention to the grill. "Working on three orders. Can you man the sides?"

I give him a two-finger salute. "I'm on it, boss."

I catch him smiling softly as I pass by him to get to the fridge. We work well together after all these years, recognizing each other's body language and anticipating each other's movements through the kitchen. We're like a well-oiled machine when we're both in our element like this.

I'm not mad at him for holding onto what he knows, especially when I see him working so hard to maintain the restaurant he's worked so hard to establish. But at times, I feel a little pinch of emotion in my stomach, an itch to try something new and show him that change can be a good thing sometimes.

But right now, I just want to relish the easy buzz of the kitchen, where it's just the two of us working together and doing what we love.

CHAPTER 10

Travis

The first couple of floral deliveries are unexpected, but by the tenth, I'm completely in shock at everyone's thoughtfulness. As the day goes on, every fifteen or twenty minutes another delivery comes. By 5:00, my aunt's room is practically stuffed to the ceiling with flowers and balloons, all with cards wishing her well. It smells like a garden, and the brightly colored petals make the gray walls less dismal.

Around 6:00, the nurses return Aunt Nadine to her room with good news. Her hip surgery went well. She'll be asleep for a while recovering from the surgery. They'll continue to monitor her and then assess her for next steps regarding her stroke. She'll likely have to start physical therapy for both the hip injury and the stroke, and she'll also see a speech pathologist. It will be a long road to recovery, but I'm hoping and praying that she'll be able to live without any problems and maintain her independence.

My parents are out grabbing something for dinner when a couple more deliveries arrive. My aunt is asleep in her bed, surrounded by flowers and balloons and even a couple of little keepsakes that she hasn't had a chance to see yet.

I read through a few of the cards. It seems like most of these people were students of hers at one point. I knew she was a popular teacher, but I hadn't realized just how many lives she touched in her years at the school.

My phone buzzes with a message from Gloria. She tells me not to worry about the presentation and that this family situation takes precedence. Strangely, I haven't been thinking much about the presentation for the last couple of hours, despite all the downtime I have had while I'm waiting for my aunt to wake up.

The door opens softly. "Travis?" my mom whispers. "We got dinner from the cafe, and we brought you a burger."

I stand and give my mom a hug, knowing she's still worried about my aunt. My dad takes a look around the room. "Wow. That's a lot of flowers." He hasn't been back here since he left this morning for work.

Mom smiles up at him. "Nadine is loved by so many, you know."

He puts a hand on her shoulder, nodding, and giving her a reas-suring smile. It's a nice moment between them, one I don't see enough of. Then, he hands me a brown and white striped paper bag with the Maple Falls Cafe logo on the front. It reminds me of Cally, and I wonder if she was there when my parents were picking up dinner.

"It does make me wonder, though," my mom says, taking a slow lap around the room and gently touching the rose petals of a bouquet. "How did so many people find out about her stroke? I haven't spoken to anyone about it except the elementary school principal." She looks at me expectantly.

"Well, I did mention it to the woman at the baked goods tent... oh, and Luann Britzen," I explain. "She caught me earlier when I was walking through the park."

My mom brightens. "Luann! Oh, I've always liked her so much. She is so thoughtful. I bet she made sure to tell everyone."

"Is she the cheerleader who you took to junior prom?" my father asks.

My mom answers for me with an enthusiastic nod.

I shrug one shoulder. We had gone as friends, but there's no reason to point that out now. "I guess it's possible she did it." Luann never seemed like the kind of person who would be so concerned about someone else, but everyone changes. It's been a long time since I saw her.

We linger near the foot of the bed, discussing the flowers, and my aunt grunts a little in her sleep.

"Maybe we should eat out in the hall and let her get the rest she needs," my father suggests.

I gaze back at my aunt lying in the hospital bed. Besides the couple of lamps in the corner, a stream of bright fluorescent light comes in through the open door. I reach over to turn off the lamp nearest her bed, and a name on a card catches my eye—Cally Stein.

The message is so sweet; it gives me pause. "To my favorite teacher and the originator of my courage. I hope you get well soon. The school, and the art nights at the library, won't be the same without you." I smile at the card, touched by her simple but heartfelt wishes, and turn off the lamp.

We're about to head out when a nurse, a middle-aged woman in purple scrubs and cropped blonde hair, glides through the dark and looks at all my aunt's monitors. We hang around and wait for some sort of assessment.

"She'll be sleeping for a while," she says with a tight smile. "You all should go home for the night. We'll keep a close eye on her."

Mom starts to protest, but my father reminds her that she's exhausted and may as well sleep while my aunt is, so we give in and carry our dinner out to the parking lot.

On the way to our cars, my mom is still gushing over Luann's thoughtfulness. Frankly, I'm a little surprised that Luann would do something like this. It's a bit unexpected, and given the clingy way she acted today, I question her motives. But on the other hand, she and Jeremiah both came to our holiday parties and also spent time with me at Aunt Ine's house quite a bit in the summer, not to mention that she had my aunt as a teacher in school, so she knew her pretty well.

But Cally mentioned that my aunt was her favorite teacher, and it seemed like they might have some other connection with an art program, according to her card. I don't know anything about art classes at the library. I'll have to ask Aunt Ine about it once she is awake and feeling a bit better.

I follow my parents home in my rental car. Mom in her car, and Dad in his since he had to go to work. Dad is the restless type and usually has a difficult time staying in one place very long. It seems like they are often in separate cars.

When we get home, we all sit together at the dining room table, which is a rarity these days. I try to eat, but my stomach is unsettled. I'm still worried about my aunt's recovery. I can't shake the memory of her trying to reach out with her right hand and the way it felt limp when I took hold of it. What if she can't draw anymore? Art is her passion. If she loses that, I don't know how she's going to ever recover.

I push my chair away from the table. My mom stares at my half-eaten burger and untouched fries. "You aren't going to eat more? Did you even have lunch today?" she asks.

Come to think of it, aside from half this burger, the only other thing I've eaten today is Cally's pastries. But the anxiety over my aunt's condition is winning out, and I don't think I can stomach another bite.

"I'm just going to take a shower and get some rest," I tell her.

My father watches me with concern in his eyes, but he doesn't say anything. Their gazes follow me as I head down the hall.

It's still very early after I take my shower. Even though it's been a long day, I can't make myself sleep. I shift restlessly in the bed and eventually get up to try to get some work done at the desk. But I can't concentrate, so I go back to bed and open my phone.

My eyes burn from playing Sudoku on my phone for over an hour. I return to my desk, where my old sketchbook taunts me. It's at the tips of my fingers, but I can't make myself reach for it. I pick up a sketching pencil and roll it between my fingers. I really can't remember the last time I even held a pencil, let alone drew something.

I crane my head back and stare up at the ceiling. My head feels like it weighs fifty pounds, and my neck is stiff and tired from the long day. How can it feel like my mind is racing when I can't even catch a single comprehensible thought? I turn my head and stare outside. The overcast sky obscures the moon, leaving only a dark and dreary fall night.

I go over to the window and open it, and the cold air rushes in. It feels damp, like it could start raining any moment. Petrichor—that's the name of the smell when it rains for the first time in a while. I remember my aunt telling me about that years ago. I breathe in the scent. It's earthy and a little sweet... and calming. I reclaim my chair and stare out at the yard.

At some point, I manage to doze off for a few minutes. I awake to a brisk breeze that sends a chill down my bare arms. As I try to sit up, my neck cramps because of the awkward angle from my nap. I try to stretch it out with some slow circles. Then I realize my stomach is rumbling. I guess not eating anything all day finally caught up with me.

I grab my phone from the foot of my bed and check the time. My parents are asleep by now, and I don't want to make noise rummaging around in the kitchen.

I decide to take a walk to stretch my legs and hope something stays open late in this little town. Fresh food is always available in Chicago, but here, things are a little different. After closing my bedroom window, I quickly change into a fresh pair of jeans and a sweater and head out. The ground is damp, explaining that scent of petrichor.

As I'm strolling along, memories of my childhood play in my mind. Not much has changed in the years I've been gone, it seems. All the buildings are virtually the same. But I have changed, and so have the people I grew up with. I almost can't believe that Jeremiah is married with a baby on the way. I'm not sure where he lives now, but he used to live just a couple of streets over from me, so we'd walk to and from school and football practice together.

I have more good memories than bad ones of my hometown, so why did I feel such a strong urge to get out of here back then? And why do I feel a little on edge, even now?

About twenty minutes later, a beacon of hope shines through a window on the west side of the square. Something is still open. I pick up the pace as my stomach rumbles again.

The neon sign ahead flashes a little maple leaf symbol with a folded over leaf and a crooked stem. A small smile forms on my face. I know exactly where I'm headed.

1711

CHAPTER 11

It's been a long day and an even longer night. I wasn't planning to work after the bake sale, but it felt good to help my dad out. My only regret is my footwear. Twelve hours in, my knee-high boots that have done a number on my toes. They've all been squished together, and my heels ache from standing for so long.

"Thank you so much," I tell the customers at one of my current tables. "I'll be sure to check out your website. I love to support other artists, and your handmade goods look amazing."

The ladies, Mirriam and Kate, are two friends who have just started selling quilts and blankets. They're super cute talking about their risky new business venture at the ripe old age of 61. I know they had a booth at the festival today, but I missed it since I was manning mine the whole time... well, other than when I was posing for the caricature.

"And, hey, maybe you can pay us in some of those pumpkin bars!" Mirriam winks. She places a twenty on the table to cover her half of the bill but insists I keep the change.

"Speak for yourself," Kate says, standing. "Get me in on some of those caramel snickerdoodles."

"I'm a fan of the pastries, myself," says a man's voice behind me, new yet familiar.

I spin around and nearly bump into Travis, whose dark green eyes bore straight into mine. Maybe it was the sun earlier, or maybe it's the sleeplessness now, but I notice his eyes are the color of juniper, like nothing I've ever seen before. I'm temporarily stunned by them and the way he's looking at me like maybe he'd like to get to know me better.

Travis passes and makes himself comfortable in a booth in my section.

Mirriam and Kate give me a teasing wiggle of their eyebrows, nodding at Travis behind me, before giggling like a couple of school-girls and leaving me to my own devices.

I steel myself before turning back to Travis. I don't want my mind to race away with my heart now. He's probably just being polite.

"You're out late," I say as nonchalantly as possible.

He steeples his hands together and rests his chin on the point. "Well, it's an hour earlier in Chicago."

Right. I almost forgot he lives out of town.

"What about you?" he asks, looking intrigued. "Why are you working so late? Aren't you tired after being at the festival all day?"

I shrug. "Life of a go-getter, I guess."

Travis smiles lightly.

I glance over my shoulder. I still have one more table in my section that I need to take care of before I leave for the night. I gesture to them.

"I'm about to get off, but I can take your order. Can't promise everything on the menu is available this late, but I might be able to convince the chef to make you whatever you want." He arches an eyebrow, and I add in my best faux snob voice, "I know a guy."

His smile grows a little wider, causing a faint dimple to appear in his left cheek. "You'd do that for me when we've only just reconnect-ed?" he asks.

I clear my throat, taking a couple of extra seconds to find a way to sound nonchalant. "It's a preliminary favor. Everyone gets one," I say with a forced roll of my eyes.

"A consolatory favor then?" he asks. His eyes glimmer with a tease that makes me want to linger in his presence a little longer just to see what comes next. "I'm a little greedy though. It's a shame I only get one."

I don't know what to say to that, and I'm honestly a little worried I'll say something ridiculous, so I get back to business. "So, what will it be?"

He hums and picks up the menu from the edge of the table. "Does this favor have an expiration date?" He peeks up at me from under his eyelashes.

My heart does a little pirouette. That's totally not fair! He knows exactly what he's doing. "I suppose not," I mutter.

"So, if I get a classic burger now, I can cash the favor in later?"

I shrug. "I suppose. So, a burger then. With fries or tots?"

"Tots."

"Drink?"

"What do you like?"

I startle at the unexpected question. Oh, and the simultaneous appearance of his other dimple. "We have all the usual soda options, tea, and lemonade—"

"No, no," he teases, his tired eyes brightening. "What do you like?"

I glance around behind me. My mom's tilling up the register. The patrons at my other table are still eating. And Jarred is chatting with a customer. When I look back at Travis, he's watching me expectantly.

"I guess since I'm immune to caffeine, I'd go for a Coke. It's classic, sweet, and bubbly. Goes with everything."

Travis tucks the menu back in its spot. "One Coke please."

I nod and walk away, thankful to turn my back o Travis since my cheeks are flushing hot. I put in his order, and Dad declares it the last one. Then, I find Jarred and let him know that I'm going to head out soon, and he agrees to take over my remaining customer. I run over to the caffeinated beverage machine and fill up a glass to take back to Travis's table.

"Here you go," I say, sliding the cold glass onto the table. "My shift is over, so I'll leave you in Jarred's hands. He might be young, but he's very capable. Probably better than me actually." Part of me wants to linger and continue to be his server tonight, but I'm afraid I'll say something dumb.

"I doubt he's better than you." Travis smiles. Then he studies me for a moment. "Night plans?"

I almost laugh out loud. That's absurd. I don't do anything past 10:00 P.M., and I don't do anything earlier than 10:00 A.M. Of course, he wouldn't know that. I shake my head and shift on my tired feet.

"Why don't you join me, then?" he says, gesturing toward the empty seat across from him in the booth.

"Uh…."

I don't know what to make of his request. I'm a little taken aback by his forwardness. That's never really happened to me before, regardless of the reason behind the request.

"C'mon," he says, scooting the Coke to the other side of the table. "You can have my soda."

The corner of my mouth lifts without my permission. And then one word escapes my lips. "Okay."

I untie my apron and set it in the booth next to me. My pink squiggle pencil rolls out, the one with the bunny-ear eraser. It rolls on the ground, and Travis hears it fall, so he picks it up and studies it before handing it back to me. I slide into the pocket. He gives me a beaming smile and leans forward on his elbows.

"It's cute," he says with a shrug.

I flash him a thin smile and push the pencil further into the pocket of my apron.

I remember in high school he used to win awards for his sketches. He usually won all the art competitions, though once I managed to beat him. I still remember his colored pencil drawing of a scenic lake with geese flying overhead. I was struck by the realistic ripples of the water, and the way the trees looked like they were really blowing in the breeze.

"Do you still draw?" I ask.

He flinches, maybe the first sign of uncertainty I've seen in him so far. He recovers just as quickly. "Nah."

"Why not?" I ask.

He shrugs and looks down at the table. His hand flexes as if he's remembering what it's like to hold a pencil in his hand and let his imagination take over. "The thing about hobbies is that it's hard to make time for them. When I do have time, I can't find the motivation to do them. At some point, most people just never pick them up again."

I see weariness in his eyes again. He glances up at me, still smiling faintly. I want to know what this is, this mixture of exhaustion and natural luster, of guardedness and charm.

I find myself thinking about our meeting earlier. "How's your aunt doing?" I ask.

He lets out a soft sigh. "The doctor says her hip surgery went well. They'll continue to monitor her and do more tests soon to evaluate her ability to live independently. Eventually, she'll meet with a physical therapist."

I take a deep breath. "And how are you doing?"

He looks at me with a touch of confusion. "Me?"

I nod.

"Honestly, I'm a little worried about her," he says, leaning back in the booth. "We'll know more after her evaluation, but her drawing hand was affected. Art is what she lives for."

It's sad to think that something she's so passionate about could be taken away so suddenly and without her control. I understand why Travis is worried.

"What about you?" I ask, not wanting the conversation to get too intense. "What do you live for? You work for some big company now, right?"

Travis interlaces his fingers. "Ah, work. Right. I mean, I guess I enjoy it. It earns me a living, anyway. I think I could be CEO in a few more years."

There's something lackluster in his response, as impressive as it might be. Maybe he's just upset about his aunt. And it's obvious he's tired, too.

Just then, Jarred comes by to deliver his order. Travis says thank you and closes his eyes in silence for a few seconds before taking the burger in both hands and chomping a big bite out of it. While he's chewing, he gestures to the soda still sitting untouched between us. When he swallows, he adds, "I said join me, not sit here and watch me eat." He moves his plate to the middle. "Have some tots. Or are you tired of eating your dad's cooking all the time?"

I laugh, but it comes out a little sour. "These are his recipes that I love. And besides, nobody could ever tire of these classics." I pop a tot into my mouth. It's perfectly warm, slightly crunchy on the outer layer and softer inside.

"What are your recipes like? Do you just bake, or do you have another specialty?" Travis asks before taking another bite.

His question makes me a little giddy. Aside from with Autumn and Ivy, I don't really get to talk about my recipes much. My dad still won't try new ideas, and my mom wants to be supportive without stirring the pot. It's not like I'm in competition with my dad or anything, but I wish he'd be a little more open and let me share my recipes once in a while.

"I like to take ordinary dishes and… jazz them up," I say, complete with a jazz hands gesture.

His eyes wrinkle a little at the corners. He raises his eyebrows as if he's waiting for more information, so I give it to him.

"For instance, everyone loves a classic burger," I gesture to his food. "But I like to add a little something unexpected…."

The next thing I know, I've rambled so long, Travis is at the end of his burger. He's even finished off the tots and the Coke I slid his way when he looked thirsty. I look over his shoulder at the clock. Have I just been spouting nonsense for the last fifteen minutes?

"Oh, my gosh, why did you let me talk so long?" I say, staring at him incredulously. "Why would you put up with that?"

He laughs, and it washes over me like a warm ocean wave. "I'm enjoying your enthusiasm," he tells me, leaning back and crossing his arms. He has such a steady stare, it unsettles me in the best way. "You really like cooking, huh?"

I nod bashfully. But I'm aware that I've been the center of attention for too long, so I ask him another question. "What about you? Isn't there something that makes you want to talk someone's ear off for fifteen minutes?"

A crooked smile lights his face. "I guess I used to be that way with drawing. My aunt and I would sit outside and talk technique until our tongues were tied. We didn't even need to be holding pencils."

He seems lost in thought. I pull my pencil out of my pocket and slide it over to him. "So, talk to me," I say.

He seems a little pensive at first, but a slow smile unfurls that stirs up a little ember in my chest. He picks the pencil up and turns it over in his hand a few times. "Talk about what?"

I glance around the restaurant for inspiration. It's all familiar to me, but I want to know about something new. "How about Chicago?"

"Do you have a sheet of paper?" he asks.

Arching my eyebrows, I tear a sheet off my order pad and lay it on the table. He flicks his eyes up at me for a moment, then he starts talking. "First," he says, touching the pencil to the paper and making a couple of long strokes. "I'd start with places, the buildings and the signs. There's this fun little pizza joint on the Riverwalk I liked to go to with outdoor seating and a patio where people can play games like corn hole and jumbo Jenga."

I watch as his pencil strokes rough out the scene. It's soothing the way his movements are effortless and confident, and his voice is silky and sweet like a chocolate mousse. I lean my chin on my fist and take it all in.

He talks me through the structure of the buildings and the dimensions. He folds in the background, a night sky with speckles of stars and a slim, crescent moon.

"Then there are the people," he tells me. He's so focused. I note the way his eyes squint slightly as he measures his marks carefully, and the way he chews on his lower lip as he configures the atmosphere and the movement of the people in the foreground, their arms swaying, their heads tilted back laughing, even a dog's tails wagging.

I feel like I've been watching him for hours, but the moment is quick. I know Travis is done by the way he sets the pencil down and leans back, folding his hands in his lap. I take the liberty to pull the image to my side of the table, carefully missing the droplets from the condensation from his soda.

The sketch is beautiful. I want to frame it. I've never been to Chicago, but this scene makes me want to go. Is this what the world looks like through his eyes, all of this movement and attention to detail? He includes everything down to the buttons on these people's coats and the gleam in the dog's eye, the glow of the streetlight and the moths illuminated underneath it.

"How is this even possible?" I ask, holding it up like it's been made with a pure kind of magic. "How come you never draw when you're so talented?"

He twiddles his thumbs. "It's hard to find success in art. Starving artists are starving for a reason. I just want to do something worthwhile."

I twist my mouth. "I guess that all depends on your definitions of success and what you think is worthwhile."

Behind me, I hear a deep-throated cough. I glance over at my father, who is obviously telling me to get a move on so we can close up for the night.

I climb out of the booth. Without asking, I hold the image to my chest. "I'll be keeping this," I say matter-of-factly, "because I think it's beautiful and worthwhile."

Travis studies me. I'm starting to like the feel of this. "All right then. It's yours."

I bite back a smile. "Also, my dad wants to close, so you better get out of here in the next two minutes, or he'll tell us to charge you for refills."

He stands, accidentally brushing my elbow. "Then maybe we should meet again another time when your dad isn't subtly rushing me out. Maybe I can take you to dinner somewhere that you don't probably eat every single day."

The heat in my cheeks speaks before I get the words out. "I'd like that. Here's my number."

2616

CHAPTER 12

It starts to drizzle just as I approach my parents' front yard. The light kiss of rain on my cheeks sends a shiver through my chest and arms. It feels nice, like a refreshing reset

Since my unexpected dinner with Cally, my body has been abuzz. She has a certain kind of playful, inquisitive spirit that intrigues me. I like watching her and her expressions. I like finding unique things about her, like how she has specks of brown in her otherwise bright blue eyes, kind of like the cedar waxwing's eggs I've drawn many times. Come to think of it, she has the same salient, bold kind of beauty as a cedar waxwing, which has soft feathers with a striking black mask.

I laugh to myself. What would she think if she knew I was comparing her to a bird? Would she be offended, take me seriously, or laugh it off? I want to know what kind of person she is. I want to learn more about what makes her tick. And after having a taste of her pastries and listening to her talk about cooking for the better half of twenty minutes, I want to taste more of the food that is her passion.

She makes me reconsider my passions. I told her that hobbies are something we can lose or put on the back burner, but I can tell from her, and I know from my aunt, that our hobbies and our passions can also give us life. And, heck, I drew for the first time in eight years tonight. Honestly, I loved it. I loved getting lost in the scene in my mind while also bringing it to life on the paper in front of me—in this case, a piece of her order pad. And the way Cally took it so carefully… she really thinks it's something special.

Walking up the path to the front porch, I let some of the cold drizzle soak into my skin, allowing the whirl of thoughts and emotions to settle like a rush of falling leaves. As each one grounds itself, I find my eyes getting heavier. Exhaustion creeps back in. It was easy to forget about the day I've had when I was with Cally, but now, it's weighing me down.

I step onto the front porch and shake off some of the moisture in my hair, the drops landing on the colorful fallen leaves sprinkled over Moms welcome mat. I smile, letting the happiness being home brings settle into my bones.

Opening the door as quietly as possible, I head toward the back hallway quickly, suddenly more eager than ever to get to my old bedroom. I'm home—where I can truly be myself and not have to worry about making a good impression on my boss—or anyone.

The bedsprings creak as I plop down onto the mattress, my feet hanging off the end. I wrestle a pillow under my arms and bury my face in the cool cotton pillowcase. Even though I'm still dressed, I'm about to doze off when my phone buzzes in my pocket.

I assume it's Gloria. She hasn't texted me much today, but last I heard, she thought she'd managed to push off my meeting for a week. Maybe Mr. Erkin preferred to wait until I was back to do it in person. My stomach sinks a little at the thought.

I grab my phone and swipe open the screen. To my pleasant surprise, it's a text from Cally. When she'd given me her number, I'd been more than a little flustered, especially with her dad there glaring at me. I wasn't sure if it was because I was keeping them open later than usual or because I'd just asked his daughter out. Either way, I couldn't blame him.

"Do you have anything in mind for tomorrow night?' her text reads.

Honestly, I haven't thought past wanting an excuse to see her again. I feel like I should take her somewhere special. Maple Falls Cafe is special in its own right, but I want to take her somewhere where she can experience something different, like she loves to do with her own cooking.

'I will in a moment,' I text back.

I spend about ten minutes doing a thorough Internet search for nearby restaurants. I have to sift through a lot of burger joints and pizzerias, but I finally find something I think will be fun for both of us.

'I got it,' I tell her.

Within a few seconds, she responds. 'That was a long moment. Good thing I wasn't holding my breath.'

I smile into my phone's screen. On top of being beautiful and intriguing, she's funny. When I least expect it, she surprises me with something quirky.

I send her the details for a nice French bistro in the nearby town of Grant. It's a short but sometimes necessary drive to get out of the small-town life and get into something a little more diverse and upscale.

Cally replies with a thumbs up and a cheesy smile emoji.

'Sweet dreams,' I text her.

And before I go and send some cringy sleep-deprived message about how I hope I'll dream of her smile, I toss my phone under the bed and turn off the lamp. Within seconds, I'm out.

WHEN I FINALLY RETURN TO THE WORLD OF THE COHERENT AND LIVING, the sun is already busting in between the curtains. I blink a few times.

Why does it seem three times brighter than usual? I slept like a rock... no, like a boulder.

Maybe I slept a little too well. My body feels heavy as I push myself up out of bed. How could I sleep so hard after being so exhausted? I can't blame it on the one-hour time zone difference. With the grace of a rockslide, I step onto the floor and search for my phone under the bed. There are a couple of shoeboxes under here and a plastic bin of old art supplies. I ignore them and grab my phone.

Dang, I have fifteen messages. Unfortunately, none of them are texts from Cally, and all of them are emails from Gloria and Mr. Erkin about this presentation. My boss sympathizes with me for the stress my family is going through, but he reminds me of my limited PTO and wants to know how soon I expect to be back. Gloria has done her best as my assistant to answer all questions on my behalf, which I'm eternally grateful for. I suddenly don't know how to respond. I don't know when I expect to be back. I don't know when I want to come back.

I close out my emails and head for the shower.

While I'm under the warm water, I think about my predicament with work. It melds into blips of my conversation with Cally the night before. There's no denying the stark difference between our reactions in talking about work and passions. While she lit up and seemed fueled by her job, I downplayed mine, summarizing it in a couple of broken sentences, wanting to move on to the next topic.

While my goal has always been to land a successful job at an organization where I would eventually be the CEO, I have to admit that it has been exactly that: a goal, not a passion.

Cally got me thinking about drawing again. It was always the thing I did to make myself feel better, to create beautiful scenes when I was overwhelmed by everyone's expectations. But there's no way I could make a living doing that kind of thing. It just isn't realistic. But maybe I could afford to do it once in a while. I don't know....

By the time I make it into the living room and catch sight of the clock, it's almost eleven. I hadn't paid attention to the time when I was reading those emails earlier. I slept much longer than usual. I probably haven't had deep sleep like that since Christmas break in high school. At least the lingering exhaustion from earlier has dissipated.

I walk through the house, but it's eerily quiet, which means my mother must not be home. There's no doubt my dad is working. I grab my phone and give my mother a call.

She picks up almost immediately. "Travis? I guess you finally woke up."

I clear my throat. "Yeah. I guess I was sleeping pretty hard."

"I noticed," my mother says. She sounds a little different today. There might be some lingering irritation with me, though I still don't know why. She seems calmer now. "I almost woke you up before I left for the hospital, but, well, you're not a kid anymore."

I never was, I want to say. I'm not sure why the thought pops up, but I don't want it in my head, let alone rolling off my tongue.

"How's Aunt Ine doing? Is she awake?" I ask instead. I walk into the kitchen and fill up a golden-colored vintage glass with tap water and down it in three big gulps.

"She was earlier, but the doctors did some tests that tired her out. She just fell back asleep a little bit ago."

I lean my back against the counter and cross my free arm over my chest. "I'll come by—"

"No, hun. That's okay. She'll be sleeping. You should take the rest of the day for yourself. Why don't you just plan a visit for tomorrow when she's more alert?" she tells me, cutting me off.

"But is Dad—"

She interrupts again. "He's coming by to bring me some lunch. Don't worry about us, okay? I know in the past I—" The line falls silent. For a moment, I think the call dropped, but soon her voice is back, clear as day. "Anyway, just focus on resting. Catch up on work stuff or whatever it is you're missing back in Chicago. We'll see you later."

How strange. Usually, my mom wants me to be there all the time, especially when my father isn't. But she's telling me to spend time by myself. It's unexpected, to say the least. And what would I even do all day?

"All right," I reply, a little stunned. "I guess I'll see you guys later, then. Just let me know if there are any changes. Okay?"

My mother sighs. "I will. I promise. I know how important your aunt is to you."

She hangs up before I can pull the phone from my ear. I stand quietly in the kitchen, propped up against the cabinets, totally unsure about how to fill my time. I'm not due to meet Cally for another six hours. Mom has all but asked me not to go to the hospital.

I decide to find Jeremiah on my socials and shoot him a message. It would be nice to catch up with him, maybe over lunch or a walk or something.

He messages back about fifteen minutes later, accepting my invitation for a meetup. I hurry to get dressed in a pair of jeans and a hoodie. I jog through the colorful fallen leaves out to my rental car, a little jazzed to hang out with my old buddy. I'm excited to hear about what he's been doing for the last couple of years.

For some reason, I feel like I really need to know what I've missed.
1847

CHAPTER 13

Cally

Choosing an outfit from my closet is sometimes like staring into the sun. With the right eye protection, one might be able to take a gander, but if one braves a glance on a whim, a person might go blind. Well, I attempted to tackle today's task of finding the perfect date outfit with my eyes wide open, and now I'm so blinded by all the choices that it's hopeless.

I consider FaceTiming Autumn or Ivy for advice, but I think they're both busy doing normal people things. Autumn is with Lukas, and Ivy is supposed to help around the inn today. So, I'm left to my own devices, which is frightening at this particular moment.

There's a mountain of clothes on my bed—pants, skirts, sweaters, and dresses. I think I've tried every combination of clothing items that I own, which has given me hundreds of options.

And none of them look right.

I stare at myself in my full-length mirror. I haven't touched my hair or makeup yet. Any sane person knows they should pick out the clothes first, then vibe with the outfit to see which hairstyle looks best, and finally, coordinate the eye makeup and blush color to the accents. So, that means my hair is in its natural state: semi-frizzy, wavy only in the last five inches, the part that can't decide which way it wants to go. And my face is bare, with a tinge of radish purple under my eyes from staying up an extra couple of hours last night excited about my date... and trying to plan this very outfit.

My current selection is simple compared to my usual taste. I've donned something Autumn-inspired, basic but classy: a pair of barrel jeans, loafers with pink frilly socks, and a pink cardigan over a fitted white tank. It is cute, but I don't know that it feels like me.

I'm a little worried that if I go all out on an outfit that suits me, Travis won't take me seriously. That's the theme of my whole life: the wilder the outfit, the less serious people think I am.

Or maybe I'm just nervous about this date because it's exactly that —a date. With Travis! And what's scarier is that I think I could really like him. We talk so easily, and while he might not have relinquished every detail of his life to me right off the bat, I think he's been pretty open and honest with me. That's a sign of a truly good man. And he listened to me when I talked about cooking—and he seemed to be interested. He also didn't shy away when I teased him a little. Not to mention he's got a jaw that could sharpen rocks and eyes that make me want to melt like butter in a hot skillet. And his smile….

I clutch my chest, literally, like in a high school rom-com from the early 2000s. It's such a strange feeling. I've never felt so excited and so nervous at the same time before.

"You know what?" I tell myself, pointing at my reflection. "The best version of the girl in the 2000s rom-coms is always their original selves, so that's who I'm going to be!"

I turn on an Alanis Morissette song and dive back into my clothes, chanting a mantra to inspire my choice. I am bright. I am cute. I am confident. I am creative!

With this newfound perspective in mind, I'm able to fashion a nice date outfit in ten minutes. I've opted for my 90s denim ankle-length dress with a lacy long-sleeved shirt underneath, and my favorite ombre blue sweater with the patch stars, oversized stitching, and baggy sleeves. I add a tan-colored velvet choker and a dainty silver moon necklace. For foot ware, I go for my chunky black boots, and even though no one will see them, my bright blue checkered socks. I put my hair up in a mess—but cute—bun and leave out some wispy bangs and intentional flyaways to give it a more effortless look. For the makeup, I keep it relatively simple, but with a wicked wing and a nice purple eyeshadow that makes my blue eyes look brighter. I let the freckles on my nose shine through a light foundation and finish up with a touch of rouge on my cheeks.

I give my reflection in the bathroom an affirmative nod. "Let's get it, girl."

I'M PRACTICALLY THRUMMING WITH EXCITEMENT WHEN I SEE A NAVY-blue Challenger pull into my driveway. I step out onto my porch, which is still decked out with Halloween decorations, and at the same time, Travis is exiting his rental car.

He sees me, and a smile lights up his face. "You look great," he says.

At the same time, I say, "Nice ride."

He strides over to me and up the first couple of steps until he's just a little less than eye level with me, doing an obvious but welcome once over. "I like your outfit," he says. Then there's a mischievous gleam in his eye. "Of course, as beautiful as you are, you could wear an old potato sack and look lovely."

The blush is immediate, and so is my response of looking down at the ground and trying to step past him to hide. I raise a hand to cover my face, involuntarily. He can't just leave me speechless in the first thirty seconds! It's not fair!

He lets out a deep, throaty laugh and grasps the hand that's partially covering my face, peeking around. "Is it too much? Should I keep my thoughts to myself?" he teases.

I bite a smile back and shake my head. "Maybe only half the time."

He gives my hand a soft, slow squeeze before letting it go. "I can work with that."

I clear my throat and try to strengthen my resolve. "You look great, too, by the way." He's wearing a pair of gray slacks and a fitted quarter-zip white sweater. Over the years, he's maintained his athletic look—lean but muscular, with wide shoulders. My eyes linger on his bright eyes before trailing down to his smile.

When I make it back to his eyes, a knowing twinkle glimmers at me. He totally just watched me look him over. I pretend to be unfazed even though my stomach is flipping flapjacks.

"Shall we head out then?" I ask. I step down but almost miss the last step. Thankfully I catch myself, but I also catch the feeling of his hand on my shoulder.

"Falling for me already?" he whispers.

I shoot him a glare, but it only wins me another throaty laugh. I feel like a bit of a fool, but in a good way.

He opens the door of his rental for me, gets in, and he adjusts the heat so I won't get cold.

"Buckle up," he tells me before backing out of the driveway. I look down, realizing I'd forgotten to do so, being so caught up in him.

There's something in the way he pays attention to my needs that intrigues me. He's the perfect gentleman. He doesn't try too hard, but he's not aloof.

As we drive along to Grant, we talk about the one thing I know we have in common: Maple Falls, and more specifically, Maple Falls High School. A lot of what he tells me, I already know, while what I tell him is mostly new.

I know he was a wiz-kid/jock combination who excelled in all things art and was ever-charming. He didn't know I was also an art club member or a nerd. He notes that I used to color my hair and wear interesting clothes, and that's about all he can recall about me. But I'm not surprised by that since we ran in totally different circles in high school.

"I think everyone had a crush on you back then," I tease him as we're getting out of the car. He rushes around to my side to open the door, and since the car is a little low to the ground, he reaches out a hand to pull me up.

"Surely not," he replies. It truly doesn't seem like he believes me, so he might be the type that doesn't really know how amazing everyone thinks he is.

"Everyone notices Travis Thatcher," I say with a duck of my chin and raised eyebrows.

He says nothing to that right away, instead jutting his elbow out so I can hook my arm through as we make our way inside Esquisse French Cuisine. He gives his name for our reservation, and the hostess walks us to our table in the back.

"And what about you?" he finally asks. "Aren't you aware of all these eyes on you?"

I glance around. Maybe a couple of people look quickly down at their plates, but I can't prove that they were looking at me.

"They're probably wondering what the two of us are doing together." I pinch his arm lightly. "Or maybe they're just looking at my clothes. I do get that sometimes. I mean, like you said, I used to dress kind of strangely, according to everyone else. I still like to play around with clothes and probably wear outfits some people find quirky."

I touch my velvety choker and try not to think about the leers of my teenage years.

Travis is quiet as the hostess takes our coats, then, like the gentleman he is, he pulls out my chair. While he's behind me, he leans close to my ear. "I, for one, love your quirkiness."

I'm grateful to be wearing long sleeves because I'm afraid the goosebumps on my neck and arms would be all too obvious otherwise.

Travis helps push my chair in and then seats himself directly across from me. He plants his forearms on the table, interlaces his hands in a steeple like he did last night at the cafe, and looks at me attentively.

I really don't want to talk any more about my 'quirkiness,' but I don't want our dinner to start off sour by refusing to breech a subject he wants to delve into. I shift a little uncomfortably and look away from his intent gaze.

"So, tell me, Cally," he says, picking up his menu and glancing over the top of it with a bright, interested look.

He's going to do it. He's going to delve into the one topic I kind of hate.

"What do you think I should get?" he asks instead. "I've never had French food before."

The spot knotting up in my chest immediately unravels. I'm so immensely grateful, I gasp. Trying to keep my composure, I pick up my menu, too, hiding behind it. "Let me take a look."

He lets out a soft chuckle that has my heart clenching again.

After studying the menu for a while, I discover that I'm not very familiar with a lot of these dishes. I've heard of them or seen them in movies, but there are several I've never tried. French cuisine is decidedly different from American.

Glancing up at Travis, I almost laugh out loud at the look on his face. His eyebrows are pinched together so closely, they could hold a penny. "They serve raw meat with a raw egg? Is that even legal?" he mutters.

I stifle a giggle and press his menu down so I can see the rest of his face. His mouth is fighting a full-on frown.

"So, I take it you didn't look at the menu before choosing this place?" I tease.

He meets my eyes and shrugs. "I thought you'd like it since it's different, but it's a little more different than I was prepared for. You've got to help me out."

He truly looks desperate. It's kind of adorable.

"Do you like seafood?" I ask.

"As long as it doesn't still have its eyes or the ability to move," he says seriously.

I pinch my lips together to avoid smiling or laughing. "Okay. What about beef and veggies?"

He gives me a thumbs up, and my smile cracks. "I think I know what to get you then."

Over our dinner—boeuf bourguignon for the first-timer, blanquette de vau for me, and a few scallops to share—we talk about food.

What he describes as his favorite foods sounds a lot like a high schooler's taste. Burgers, pizza, and chicken, mostly.

"So, you don't cook often, then?" I ask.

He shakes his head bashfully. "I always thought it would be cool to be that guy who can cook anything for his wife so she doesn't have to make super all the time, but I'm afraid I haven't been practicing."

I gulp down a bit of ice water and try to gloss over the fact that he basically just told me he intends to get married someday—not to me, specifically, obviously, but still....

"Well, I can teach you a few things if you want to get some practice in," I say into my plate. I'm a bit afraid to meet his eyes right now, what with the admitted goal of being an amazing husband to someone, someday.

"I'd love that," he tells me, and I look up enough to catch his lopsided grin.

We finish our meal, and Travis continues being perfect by taking care of the check. When we get outside, the sky is navy and purple, stars winking down at us. We walk back to his car, unhurried, but before he opens the passenger side door for me, he glances down the sidewalk and back up to me.

"So, I know we only planned dinner, but what do you think about extending our evening together?" he asks, his eyes lingering on my scarlet cheeks.

I nod, trying to conceal my schoolgirl giddiness at his suggestion. He takes my hand and pulls me back onto the sidewalk gently.

"I see a movie theater right down there. Want to check it out?" he asks.

"Yes," I respond breathlessly.

He keeps hold of my hand as we make our way to the theater, where we opt for a drama. To my admitted disappointment, Travis doesn't hold my hand during the movie. He does, however, lean over just enough that our elbows touch. And when I sniffle back a cry halfway through at the way the main character has nearly lost everything, he gently knocks his knee into mine and keeps it there.

By the time we get out, it's almost 10:00. We've been together for hours, but I still don't want the night to end. It's my turn to think of an excuse to stay together.

"Travis," I say, tugging on his coat sleeve. "Look, there's an ice cream shop down there that's still open."

He peers down at me. "Oh, so you're one of those people who still eats ice cream when it's freezing outside?"

I whack him playfully on the arm. "It's not that cold!"

He beams a smile down at me. "Let's go get some, then."

I almost break into a cheer, not just because I love a good scoop of ice cream, but because our time together will last that much longer. We stroll slowly down the sidewalk, past shops still decorated with pumpkins and scarecrows, and take our time eating our ice cream cones. We talk about anything and everything, and the conversation continues to be easy and fun.

When it's past 11:00, Travis sighs and says we should head back. I know we should, but I don't want to. I get the sense he feels the same way.

Regardless, we stroll back over to his rented Challenger and head for Maple Falls.

On the way back, Travis plays some lo-fi soulful music on the radio, and we listen in comfortable silence. Outside, the autumn trees shed their leaves, moving toward winter, but in here, I'm nice and cozy, warmed by his presence.

CHAPTER 14

THE ENGINE HUMS, AND EVERY ONCE IN A WHILE, I GLANCE OVER AT Cally, who is sleeping soundly in the car on the way back from our hours-long date. Her lips are slightly parted, and her breathing is soft and even.

I park in front of her house and let the car run. I'm enjoying the music and her presence, but I try to wake her a few times, and she only lets out little hums in response. Now, I'm wondering if it's okay to just give her a light tap on the shoulder.

Finally, I do so, but that doesn't wake her, so I get out and open the passenger door, crouching down outside the vehicle. I'm surprised that the sudden rush of cold air blowing in doesn't do more than make her turn her head away and give a gentle, displeased grunt.

"Cally?" I call. She rolls her head back toward me and mumbles, her eyes still closed.

I brush back a strand of hair that is strung across her eyelashes, grazing my fingertips across her forehead tenderly. She looks so sweet and beautiful, I really don't want to wake her up, but I can't leave her sleeping out here forever. She needs to go inside and get some real rest.

"Cally, wake up," I tell her, slightly louder, placing my hand on hers and giving a little squeeze. "You're home now. Don't you want to sleep in your bed?"

Her eyes slowly flutter open, heavy with sleep. Then she reaches out and touches my cheek. I hold my breath and resist the urge to lean in and kiss her right now. After all, she's just woken up and might not realize what's happening, and that wouldn't be fair.

A moment later, after her hand has fallen onto my shoulder and down my arm, she blinks a couple more times, finally waking up—a bit. "What are you doing?" she asks, sitting up quickly.

I release her hand, even though every part of me wants to keep holding it. "I'm trying to wake you up, Sleeping Beauty."

Cally laughs in a way that means she thinks I'm the silly one. "Am I home already?"

I nod.

"Oh," she says, and her lips turn down slightly.

I'm not going to lie; it fills me with joy to see that little bit of disappointment she's showing about the night finally being over. It means she wants to stay with me longer. I feel the same.

"Come on," I tell her. "I'll walk you to your door."

She climbs out of the car, almost forgetting her little bag, but I grab it for her. When it's time to go in, she lingers in the doorway and mutters a very cute, "Thank you for a wonderful night."

"I'll see you again soon," I promise her.

THE NEXT MORNING, EVENTS FROM THE NIGHT REPLAY IN MY MIND AS I get ready to go see my aunt at the hospital. My mother says that she's more alert now, and she's been able to rest a bit since her surgery.

"Aren't you going?" I ask my mother. She's still sitting at the breakfast nook in her pajamas and house slippers, sipping a cup of steaming coffee.

"I'll join you later," she tells me. "Why don't you spend some one-on-one time with Nadine? Your dad and I will come by later during lunch."

I nod and start to head back to my room for shoes and a jacket. But there's a voice in the back of my head that's nagging me about something that has me lingering in the hallway. "Mom?"

"Yes?" she asks, looking through the steam of her coffee.

I look her over, not sure what I'm searching for. "What about you, Mom? Are you doing okay, you know, with everything that's been going on?"

She pastes on a smile that doesn't quite reach her eyes. "Sure, hun. The scariest part is over now. Everything will be fine."

I'm not sure how to take her answer, but I also don't know what else to say. So, I walk away, get my things, and go.

AUNT INE IS CERTAINLY MORE ALERT WHEN I ARRIVE. SHE'S SITTING UP as much as her hip cast allows, and her face lights up when I walk through the door.

"Travis!" she cheers. Her voice is clearer than I was expecting, which is good, but there's still a hint of a slur in her words, and they come out more slowly than before. "I was hoping you'd come by soon."

I rush to her bedside, kiss her cheek, and pull up a chair. "How are you feeling?" I ask.

She gives a small wave with her left hand. "I'm fine, darling. Don't you worry."

"What'd they say?" I ask hesitatingly. "You know, about your hand?"

Aunt Ine shrugs. "It's inconvenient, but I'm just happy to be here."

My heart squeezes. How can she be so positive about this?

She studies me for a moment, her eyes not as clear as they usually are and drooping slightly with exhaustion. After a long silent moment, she smiles. "I haven't seen you in so long. You look good."

I bow my head to avoid her gaze. "I'm sorry. I know I haven't been calling as much lately. And since I haven't come back for the holidays recently—"

"Well, you're here now. And I'm so happy to see you."

Aunt Ine, despite the stroke and spending days sedated in the hospital, looks almost like she always has, save for her tired eyes. Her hair is a sandy blonde like mine, though hers has paled with age. We have similar green eyes, though mine are a bit darker. And despite the season, we share a similar olive skin tone. When I was young, people would sometimes assume she was my mom because we look so similar. My mother is also blonde, but her hair borders on light brown, and she has my grandfather's brown eyes.

After I dodge specific questions about how work is going, Aunt Ine asks what my plans are.

"What do you mean?" I ask.

"Are you still planning to be CEO in the next few years, or is there something else you're working toward?" she asks.

I should have known she'd be asking these kinds of life questions after not speaking to her for so long. "I'm not sure," I tell her.

It's true. All I've really been focused on is getting a dependable, successful job and moving up the ladder. Though I thought I'd balanced my life well in Chicago, coming back to Maple Falls has me realizing that none of my friends have reached out to me since I left, and I've never even tried to stay in touch, even with good friends like Jeremiah.

"Are you… still drawing?" my aunt asks. I can tell by the saddened look in her eyes that she probably already knows the answer.

"No. Well, actually—"

I recall the other night in the cafe with Cally when I used her wonky pink and purple pencil to sketch out the Chicago skyline. That was the first time in years that I've put a pencil to paper in that sense. "I drew a picture on the back of an order pad a couple of nights ago."

Aunt Ine cocks her head slightly. "Is that right?"

A faint smile creeps across my face. Cally makes me see the world so differently. She makes me want to try harder to find true happiness. She inspires me.

"You look awfully fond of that order pad drawing," Aunt Ine leads. "It must have had a very pleasing outcome."

It did feel good to draw again, and I was mostly pleased with the quick sketch. If I had a proper drawing pencil and some good paper, I could have done much more. But I can't deny that the real reason for the smile is the person I was drawing for.

"Unless there's something else," she prods tenderly. "Perhaps it's about who that order pad belongs to?"

"Actually, yeah," I say, mustering up the courage to open this can of worms. Aunt Ine has been bugging me for years to find a nice girl to keep me company in the big city. "I had a date that went really well."

"Oh! Who was it? Someone from here?" my aunt asks.

"Cally Stein," I explain. "I think she is a couple of years younger than me."

"Cally?" Her face lights up, and it's clear she knows exactly who I'm speaking of. "Her family owns the cafe. And of course, I had her as a student years ago. She was always so bright. Had a great eye for art at such a young age. I think she comes to my painting class once in a while even now, though I haven't spoken to her much. She seems lovely."

I'm pleased with my aunt's reaction. "She is. I really like her. But I didn't know she was into art, too. I guess we might not have spent much time on that topic because of me... and my aversion to drawing."

"Is it an aversion now?" Aunt Ine asks, her eyebrows nearly touching. "Why is that?"

I don't want to upset her. And maybe "aversion" isn't the right choice of words anyway. "It's not an aversion, per se," I correct myself. "I just don't want to waste my time on something that will only distract me from my goals."

My aunt half-crosses her arms. The effect isn't the same as it used to be since she can't properly move her right side. "Oh, so it's a waste of time?"

I bite my tongue. "I didn't mean it like that. It's just that I... well, I don't really want to talk about this right now. I'm sorry for using those words. That was insensitive of me."

Aunt Ine lets out a long sigh. "Listen," she says. Her voice has a new shakiness to it. "This stroke is going to change everything for me. I don't know how I'll recover or if I'll fully recover. It will certainly affect my art either way. And you know how much art means to me. I thought we were the same in that sense."

Her words leave me speechless for a moment. We are the same in that way, or at least we were. I don't want to discount her love of art even if I'm struggling to find a place for it in my life. I don't want to discount the time we spent together when I was growing up because she taught me so much.

"You can learn to use your right hand again," I tell her firmly. "You're strong. Or you can use your left hand."

Aunt Ine shakes her head. "I don't know, Travis. I won't be able to get the details right. It won't be the same."

"Then maybe you take a new approach. Abstract?"

She smiles softly, but again, it's unconvincing because her eyes remain dull, almost lifeless. I feel bad now that I've made her sad.

"Darling," she begins, lifting her right hand just enough to set it atop my wrist. "I hope you'll never take certain things for granted. Anything can be lost in an instant with no way to get it back. Just... think about what's important to you, and make a safe space for it."

I put my hand over hers and nod.

I have a lot of thinking to do about what is really important to me.

CHAPTER 15

Cally

One week ago, I had the most amazing date of my life. Granted, I haven't dated much at all, so I don't have a lot to compare it to. But it was lovely—perfect. I'd been a little embarrassed after falling asleep in his car, but Travis said I was too precious to wake up.

I haven't seen Travis this week as much as I've wanted to because he's been spending a lot more time with his aunt. She has started physical therapy and will be adding speech therapy soon. He wants to give her all the support he can. I totally get it, and I don't want to pull him away from his family, especially at such a sensitive time. But I really want to see him again. Until then, I have to be content with the occasional text.

I look down at the last text he sent last night.

'See you later, precious,' with a kissing smiley-face emoji.

We haven't actually kissed yet, but I can't say I don't think about it every time I'm in his presence.

"It was that good, huh?" Ivy asks. "I've never seen you so... swoon-y."

Ivy and I are hanging out in the corner of my parents' restaurant kitchen brainstorming menu ideas for this year's Thanksgiving event. A holiday centered around food—hello! That's my literal purpose in life. I'm so excited. Plus, this year, I'll actually have a plus one! Travis has confirmed that he'll be staying until at least Thanksgiving, which makes me absolutely giddy. But I can't let myself think past that, not yet.

"I hope to see you swoon sometime soon," I tell her. "You deserve it. Plus, it feels absolutely divine."

Ivy rolls her eyes, but her cheeks redden slightly, just enough to make me wonder what she really thinks about dating someone. She's had a boyfriend or two, but it's been a while for her. I hope she gets to feel seen and loved in this special way soon.

"Well, if he isn't already in love with you, he certainly will be after he tries all of your recipes. Even if he does have a palate of a fifteen-year-old or whatever you said, I think you can make a man out of those taste buds!"

I nearly spew out my hot cocoa from laughing so hard. It's silly, but I do hope that he likes my dishes. For that matter, I hope everyone does. I put my whole heart and soul into them, trying to create something delicious and comforting that makes everyone feel full... not just physically, but emotionally as well. I want them to feel content in every way possible.

"He's going to be here later," I tell Ivy. "I haven't seen him in three days, so I'm a little nervous."

"Well, there's no need for you to be," she says, placing her hand on my shoulder like a boxing coach in the corner of the ring. "You're smart, creative, hilarious, and so kind, not to mention super hot!"

I roll my eyes but accept the compliment. Even though I like wearing fun clothes, I'm also aware that some people think it's childish or that I'm looking for attention. But Travis doesn't see it that way. He's told me he likes how I show my creativity through what I wear and how I do my hair.

Today, I'm wearing a pair of mustard yellow wide-legged jeans and a high-necked white puff-sleeve blouse with a cute paisley-patterned sweater vest over it. I've paired it with my brown plaid socks and brown fisherman sandals. I decided to keep my hair half down with a couple of braids, tying them together with a bow in the back.

My watch chirps, signifying that it's time for my shift to start. I'm helping with the lunch rush today since our waitress called in sick. The original plan was to meet Travis for lunch, but now he's coming here to see me since I can't get away.

"All right, well, I'd better suit up," I say, grabbing my apron. "It's about to get busy in here."

Ivy gives me a quick hug and leaves. It's time to get to work.

An hour later, it is still, indeed, very busy. The lunch rush can span three hours some days, especially when it's this close to the weekend. Noon, of course, is the peak. And that is precisely when Travis walks in. I've had my mom keep a table open for him, and right now, it's one of only three without customers, and the only one with no trace of the last people who sat there.

I rush over to him, suddenly aware of how warm it is in here. The back of my neck is practically sweating. I use the extra pencil from my apron to weave my hair into a bun.

"That's a neat trick," Travis says, watching me.

"Yeah," I laugh. "I should have known the lunch rush would be crazy today, but I was not prepared."

He studies me for a quick moment. "It's good to see you."

Such a simple phrase makes my insides feel like there's a trapeze artist in there, flying around and flipping back and forth.

"Will you have time to sit with me?" he asks.

I smile sadly. "I don't think I can. I'm sorry, I really misjudged—"

"Hey." He stops me by grabbing onto the tips of my fingers. "Don't worry about it. I'm just happy to see you and eat some good food."

"Okay," I say. I'm happy to see him, too, but I'm disappointed that I don't get to spend more quality time with him today.

He releases my fingers. "We'll make up for it," he assures me. "And remember, you agreed to let me help you prepare for the town's Thanksgiving luncheon."

"Yes," I confirm. "The Maple Falls Harvest Feast."

"I'm sure you'll be sick of me after that anyway," he adds, smirking.

"Impossible," I reply with a smile.

I hear the ding of the kitchen bell, signifying that an order has been completed and is ready to be taken to the table. I go ahead and take Travis's order and get back to running around the restaurant. It's definitely not my favorite part of this job, but until I can prove myself to my dad and convince him to give me more independence in the kitchen, I'll do whatever I need to do.

What gets me through is the thought of Travis and me spending time in the kitchen together. He admitted before that he's no chef, but he wants to help me in whatever way he can, and I'm so excited that we'll get to do something like that together.

A little while later, I deliver a plate to Travis with his Salisbury steak, proud that he didn't order a cheeseburger again. Maybe eating at the French restaurant made him feel like he could try new dishes.

"Thank you, Cally," he says, and I'm suddenly aware of how beautiful my name is when I hear it in his voice.

"I hope you enjoy it," I tell him before rushing off to help my other tables.

Amid the chatter of the townsfolk enjoying their lunches and the swinging of the kitchen door, I feel at peace. When I spot my dad through the kitchen order window working hard and see my mom up at the register with her genuine, winning smile plastered on, I feel like everything is right in the world. And then there are all the times I glance at Travis and find him watching me like it's his favorite thing to do, and it sends a warm tingle over me.

"How is everything?" I ask him a little while later when he's about half finished with his meal.

"It's so good," he says. Then he raises his eyebrow. "But I wonder what the Cally Special version of this would taste like."

My cheeks heat a little. "Maybe one day you'll find out."

He steeples his hands the way he often does and grins. "I look forward to it."

I leave him to his meal and send off a couple of tables that have finished their lunches. It's one of those rare occasions when the empty tables immediately get filled with new people, so I don't catch much of a break. I get a little wrapped up in a particularly difficult customer who has a bit of an attitude, but I'm not too involved to miss the exact moment Luann comes in and plops herself right next to Travis... not even on the other side of the table, but right smack next to him.

I don't know why I'm surprised when he doesn't tell her to get out or sit on the other side. Why should I expect him to treat his beautiful childhood friend that way just because we went on one date and shared a few texts this week? He is still technically single and all.

As I'm waiting on my other tables, I keep glancing at them out of the corner of my eye. I'd felt Travis's eyes on me the whole time before Luann got there, but since she seated herself beside him, I don't think he's looked at me once. Then again, Luann looks great. I mean, she always does, but I didn't know it was possible for someone to look so effortlessly cute in black leggings, Uggs, and a flannel over a T-shirt.

About fifteen minutes later, I notice that Travis's plate is empty. He's been here almost forty-five minutes. The rush is dwindling a little, but I've still got several tables in my section. I have to do my job, with or without Luann's presence.

I write up Travis's ticket and steel myself to take it to him. The nearer I get, the clearer their conversation becomes.

"Oh, uh, I guess I should thank you for making sure my aunt has lots of flowers and well wishes. Her room is flooded," he says.

Wait. What?

"Of course!" Luann doesn't miss a beat. "I mean, until she's ready for visitors at least, she'll know people are thinking of her."

She's taking credit for something I did with my friends. Sure, maybe she sent flowers, too, but Autumn, Ivy, and I were the ones who spread the word. Irritation and disgust flood my veins. And Travis seems so sure that it was her. I wonder what gave him that impression?

I decide not to say anything about it as I reach his table. I didn't do any of that for recognition. I just wanted Ms. Nadine to feel loved and cared for.

"Here's your ticket," I say without meeting his or Luann's eyes. "You can pay up at the front when you're ready."

Before he can respond, I turn around and go straight to another table. I'd rather deal with the needy customer's persistent questions than face him right now. He probably didn't even want to look at me with Luann in his presence.

A few minutes later, I'm about to do one last check on Travis, to offer a to-go drink or something, just because I feel a little rude for being short with him. Even if his attention was on Luann, it was my duty as his waitress to be patient and kind, and in that case, I wasn't.

Circling back to his table, my heart deflates a little more. He's getting up and walking with Luann to the front of the restaurant.

"I can give you a ride to the hospital," I hear him tell Luann. They must be going to see his aunt. I was hoping to get to visit her with him, but I guess not.

My eyes linger on him as he walks out of the cafe, hoping that he'll at least look back at me before he steps outside. But Luann is tugging on his arm, and they're out the door without so much as half a glance in my direction. I step over and clear off the table, finding a twenty-dollar bill and a scribble on the napkin that says, 'Talk to you later.'

It should make me feel better that at least he left this for me, but it seems strange. I'd rather he said the words to my face, or at least said them with his eyes. But maybe I'm moving back a slot in his mind.

Maybe the popular girls keep winning the guys, even after high school is over.

CHAPTER 16

Travis

THE LONGER I SPEND TIME WITH LUANN, THE MORE I MISS CALLY. THE two of them couldn't be more opposite.

I was confused by Cally's reaction in the cafe. Maybe those two have a past that I don't know about that caused Cally to close herself off, or maybe it was something else, but I could tell when Cally wouldn't meet my eye that something was wrong. I left her a note to let her know I am still looking forward to talking to her later. I hope that whatever's wrong, she feels better by then.

This afternoon is definitely not going according to plan. I wanted to have a nice lunch with Cally since we haven't been able to line up our schedules for the past three days, but then she ended up having to work. I was still happy to see her, but we didn't get to talk much since the restaurant was so busy.

Then, Luann inserted herself and practically dragged me out of there before I was ready. I'm having a hard time knowing what to do with her. This has happened before, when I was talking to Cally at her booth, not wanting to leave. Luann came in and dragged me out of the conversation. Surely, she hasn't been doing it on purpose. I don't think she's that kind of girl.

But I'm having a difficult time finding the words to tell her to give me some space. We used to be so close, after all. I don't want to brush her off or make her feel bad for caring about me and my family.

"Are you going to the Harvest Feast?" Luann asks.

We're almost to the hospital now, and she's already covered the topics of her four-year college, her hot yoga classes, her prize-winning border collie, and her high school-aged sister's boyfriend drama.

"I'm planning on it," I tell her.

She leans over the console of the car. "Should we... go together?" she asks.

"Uh...." I feel a little awkward for some reason. "I'm going with someone else."

"Oh. Jeremiah?"

I clear my throat.

Just as I'm about to answer, she waves me off. "You know what? Never mind. It's not really my business. I'm sure I'll see you there, regardless of who you're going with."

Finally, we make it to the hospital, and my parents are there. I've noticed this week that my dad has been around a little more, and my mom has been less irritable and more like her cheery, overzealous self.

Mom snatches up Luann in the first two seconds of being in the same room. "Luann! Oh, my gosh! Look at you! You're just as pretty as ever!" she squeals.

Luann laughs and clasps my mother's arms. "Oh, Mrs. Thatcher, how could you call me pretty when I'm in the same room as you! You're an ageless beauty!"

I look over at Dad like he could have some sort of explanation about why these two seem so similar. He just gives me a shrug and shoves his hands into his pockets. He's a man of few words. Maybe that's why he and my mom have managed to stay together for so long.

She doesn't have to fight him for room to speak since he gives it freely.

"Oh, Luann, I'm just so happy you're here!" Mom gushes. "I've been wanting to thank you for organizing so many people to send flowers to my sister. That was just oh, so kind of you!"

Luann bows her head humbly. "Oh, well, I'm just happy that everything turned out well." She glances around the room at the various arrangements and balloons. "This is really incredible."

I look over at my aunt, who is watching the scene unfold. Dad always tells me that she and I have the same intense stare when we're observing. It's funny how similar we are.

"Luann, so you came here with Travis, right?" my mother asks. I can tell by the way she's looking between us that she's hoping we're together, in the dating sense.

Luann shimmies over and bumps her shoulder against mine. "Well, you know how sweet Travis can be. I wanted to come see Nadine just as soon as he said she was taking visitors, and he offered me a ride."

My face quirks up in a tight smile. I guess that is the gist of it, but I felt a little more cornered into bringing Luann here rather than offering the ride, what with all her talk about feeling a migraine coming on and not being able to drive until it passes. Also, she hasn't even said hello to my aunt yet.

Slipping out of their shrill bubble, I pull up the seat next to Aunt Ine's bedside and fold my arms over the layers of blankets covering her.

"So, this isn't Cally Stein," Aunt Ine mutters to me quietly.

I can't help but laugh. "Indeed, it is not."

"Why's Luann here?" she asks.

Even though she's as good as a nun when it comes to treating everyone with respect and kindness, especially to their faces, for some reason, my aunt has always had a tough time liking Luann. She hasn't ever told me why. She's only said that she rubs her the wrong way or something vague like that. Still, she was always welcoming when Jeremiah and Luann would come hang out at her house with me.

"She, uh, wanted to see you, I guess," I tell her. "She's the one who organized all of this." I gesture around her room. A lot of the flowers are starting to shrivel now, but there are still a couple of fresh, new vases by her bedside.

"Is that right?" she asks, looking around. "I wonder what she's scheming."

I cough in surprise. "Why would you say that?"

Aunt Ine purses her lips and doesn't answer. But she does look at Luann with narrowed eyes.

It seems like Luann and my mom are deep in a conversation about this year's upcoming Christmas pageant, and Dad is sitting in a chair behind me about to fall asleep.

"Listen, I want to talk to you about what I said before, about how I feel about art," I tell my aunt.

Her suspicious glare fades, and she turns to me instead. "The part about how it's a waste of time, or the part about how you have an aversion to it even though you used to live for it?"

"You know I didn't mean either of those things," I whisper. "I just... I don't know how to feel about it anymore. And I—"

"What are you two whispering about?" asks Luann, who pops up across the bed. "Can I get in on it?"

I'm staring wide-eyed at my aunt, praying that she'll read my expression and not talk about this sensitive matter with a person like Luann. She harrumphs, literally, and then plasters on a fake smile.

"Sorry, dearie, it's between me and my nephew," my aunt tells her. "You'll have to pry it out of him yourself if you want to know."

A few minutes later, my mom offers to take Luann back into town with them. I'm hopeful that that'll leave my aunt and me some time alone to talk out this whole art thing, but Luann declines. And just like that, I'm stuck with her for almost a full hour while she attempts to butter up my aunt and flashes me a flirty smile every twenty-six seconds.

I realize the only way to get her out of here is to offer to take her home myself. How can she be so incredibly stubborn? She's got a real talent....

"Listen, I think we'd better head out, Luann," I say. "Aunt Ine's been ambushed with visitors all morning. I'm sure she'll want some time to relax. And I need to get home to, uh, take care of some things."

"Ah, really?" she pouts. "That's too bad. I'm having such a good time."

My aunt pats her hand. "Yes, dearie, I'm getting quite tired. They still have me on pain meds that make me sleepy. So, I'd like to get some rest now."

Luann smiles brightly. "Sure, Auntie. I'll come back and see you soon, then."

One thing about Aunt Ine is that she does not take kindly to people acting too familiar with her. And she's only ever been an aunt to me. She always says she doesn't have the room in her heart to be an aunt to anyone else. I always thought she was joking. But now, the look on her face is pure, although veiled, disdain.

As soon as I get Luann out to the car to leave, and she buckles herself in, she quickly turns to me. "Travis!" she shouts.

I flinch, unprepared for the sudden rise in volume right next to me. "Yes?"

"Let's go out."

I give her a quizzical stare. "I'm sorry?"

"Let's go out, like for dinner or something, just the two of us. How about tomorrow?"

All I can do for a full fifteen seconds is blink at her. Just where did she get this idea?

"I don't think so," I mutter.

She's genuinely taken aback. "What? Are you already dating someone?"

Are Cally and I dating? We went on a date. I try to talk to her every day. I think about what it would be like to kiss her or hold her hand all the time. But is it serious enough to be called dating? I'll be going back to Chicago eventually. What will happen between us then? I haven't really given it much thought. But suddenly, I very much do not want to give it any more thought because my chest aches to think about it.

"Not exactly," I tell Luann, starting the car and backing out of the parking space.

"C'mon, Travis," she presses. "You remember what it was like to be together, right? We've been best friends forever. Let's give it a shot. I know we could be good together. It's what everyone expected anyway. It's bound to happen eventually."

My stomach churns, and my throat constricts. Instead of feeling anxious, I actually feel pretty ticked off. I grip onto the steering wheel and try to keep my composure.

It's what everyone expected anyway? To heck with everyone's expectations.

"No," I say plainly. "Sorry, Luann, I just don't feel that way."

She reaches across and puts her hand on my bicep. "Trav, I think it's a mistake to pass up something that could be so epic."

I press on the gas harder, eager to get her home and out of my car. I want to be a gentleman, to politely let her down, but there's something unexpected rearing its head, and I don't know how much longer I can fight it off.

"Stop," I tell her, shaking her hand off my arm. "I don't want to date you."

"W-why?" she mutters, withdrawing her hand.

I take in a long, controlled breath and let it out. "I don't know if there was some miscommunication or if I accidentally gave you the wrong idea, but I just don't feel that way about you. I'm sorry."

"Trav—" she whimpers.

I pull into her parents' driveway and don't even put the car in park. I'm not sure if she even lives here anymore, and I don't care. "You should head inside. I need to go home."

She's looking at me with disbelief and quivering lips. "Fine," she whispers. She gets out and slams the door before running inside.

I don't linger long, just long enough to see her open the front door, then I race home.

I feel a little pent-up energy, so I go into the spare room and jog on the treadmill until I feel like I'm going to pass out, then I collapse on my bed and flip open my phone for the first time since I'd left the message for Cally that I'd see her later. To my disappointment, there are no messages from her.

Maybe she's still working.

There is also, to my disappointment, a very long list of texts and emails from Gloria and Mr. Erkin, mostly the former. I read through them absentmindedly until I get to the last one she sent.

'Do you know when you're coming back? Will you be returning soon?' the message reads. They want to do the presentation soon. I haven't looked at it all week.

I position my thumbs properly on the keyboard and type out Y-E—

But something stops me from typing the rest. I get up and go over to the window, leaving my phone on the bed. My breath fogs up the glass but dissipates within a couple of seconds.

Even though things have felt a little weird since I returned home, I've also felt more at rest than I have in a long time, other than the issue with Luann today. My childhood home is still relaxing and peaceful, despite the mixed emotions I have, or had, about staying here.

The street is lined with beautifully colored trees, most have gone deep crimson now. Piles of leaves litter the sidewalks, and in the yard across the street, a couple of young kids are jumping into a leaf pile. There's an apple tree between my parents' yard and Mr. and Mrs. Cox's that our families share. Growing up, my friends and I loved to sit down there and eat fresh apples. Sometimes, Mrs. Cox would make homemade apple sauce and apple butter. My mom would make apple juice, always explaining that it was easier than baking.

I let out a long, slow sigh. I'd always wanted to get out of here to escape the expectations of my parents, my teachers, my friends... the whole town, really. But are that many people keeping track of me? Or am I running away from nothing?

Nobody has said they are disappointed in me, not outright. And, heck, even if they did, it doesn't matter. It's my life, and I should get to decide what I do. I don't want to be backed into a corner trying to meet everyone's expectations, trying to fit their ideas of success.

And what am I doing now? In Chicago, it's the same. I want to make CEO so I don't have to live under anyone's thumb. And I thought the job would be impressive. Haven't I still been doing the very thing I've been running from, just in another city?

Maybe rushing back to climb the corporate ladder isn't what I really want. But if I don't go back, what would I do? Could I find happiness here? What if people are disappointed in me? What if I wind up right back where I started over ten years ago?

But things are different now, and there are people in my life, like Cally and Aunt Ine and probably even Jeremiah, who would support me. Right?

Especially Cally... she seems so passionate about what she does. I think I can learn a lot from her. Maybe she could be a more permanent part of life here.

I shake my head and bump it against the cool pane of glass. Who am I kidding? We've only gone out on one date. It's a little too early for thoughts like that... isn't it?

CHAPTER 17

Cally

"Travis," I say, trying to keep a neutral tone when I answer the phone. "I wasn't expecting to hear from you."

"What do you mean?" he asks, probably thinking I'm teasing him. "I promised you, didn't I? I'm not the kind of guy who makes promises he can't keep."

"Oh, right. The Harvest Feast...."

So maybe this is just about his integrity, then? He's got to fulfill his promise before he can free himself from me and be with Luann. He is a gentleman. There's no way he could be a two-timer.

"So, what's the first step in Thanksgiving preparations?" he asks, sounding perfectly cheery.

"Well, I've been working on a spread, but I guess there are a couple other non-food related things to take care of, too."

"Perfect! Maybe I'll be useful after all!" he says with a gentle laugh. I can't help but smile at the sound of it.

This is okay. We can hang out today. Even if I wanted something else to come of this, even if he chooses another girl or goes back to Chicago, I can still enjoy his company. I can bear it.

"I'll come by at eleven," he says, though it's almost eleven now.

"I still have to get together a list, so why don't you come to my house?" I suggest.

He agrees, and we hang up.

Today, I want to be comfortable, but I know I'll see Travis later. So, it's only natural that I want to be cute, too. Yet, I don't want to seem like I'm trying too hard to keep his attention. I'm wearing a pair of red gingham pants that are frilly around the cuff and a fitted white sweater with a scalloped V-neck. I've tied a silky scarf around my neck that has a sort of vintage tortoise print. My hair is piled on top of my head in a fairly delicate bun with just a few hairs to frame my face, similar to how I wore it on our date. Since I'm home, I'm also wearing my fluffy socks and my slip-on house shoes that are a little worse for the wear.

I hear the engine of Travis's Challenger, and I try not to let myself get too excited as I meet him at the door.

"Hey," he says, his smile appearing genuine. Maybe he really is happy to see me.

"Hi," I greet him back. Now, I'm overthinking how much I should smile. I didn't worry about it before, back when I thought I knew what he wanted. "Come on in."

"Wow," he says. "I finally get to check out your digs. I'm so excited." He rubs his hands together like he's about to find something truly amazing.

My house is a little eclectic, kind of like my clothes. I've got a gallery wall of pictures and bookshelves, at least five plants in every light-filled window, and a selection of thrifted, mostly vintage, furniture, including a plaid futon.

"I'm afraid there's not much to look at in here," I say, walking toward the kitchen.

I barely hear him mutter, "I beg to differ."

I turn my head just enough to sneak a peek behind me, and it seems like he's looking at me. Is he… talking about me when he says that? Ugh, I'm so confused!

"So, do you have a pair of those cozy-looking slippers for me, too?" he asks, pointing at my footwear. He slips off his shoes and puts them neatly by the door beside mine.

I chuckle. "Unfortunately, these are the only ones I have, and I don't think they'll fit you."

"Ah, maybe a Christmas present then," he says with a wink.

So, he's thinking about something a whole month away? Or is he just teasing me?

He is not helping me feel any less conflicted.

I clear a spot at the kitchen bar for him to sit, and I climb onto the barstool next to him where my pile of notebooks, magazines, and cookbooks sits. He picks up a cookbook.

"When are you going to write your own cookbook?" he asks after a minute.

Honestly, I've never thought about that before. Maybe I should. But no, that's crazy. Why would I write a cookbook when I don't even get to serve my own food? How would I know if people would actually like my recipes or not?

I give a coy shrug. "When you get your own art exhibition, I guess."

Travis laughs and bumps his knee into my leg playfully. "Fair enough, beautiful."

I gulp before my heart has the chance to hop out of my mouth. This man… he's torturing me. Does he know it?

"Let's get to business," I say, straightening out my assorted notes.

Travis scoots his barstool closer to me until our arms are flushed together, and my heart is beating erratically.

"What's wrong?" Travis whispers close to my ear. "Can't focus?"

I bite the inside of my cheek and try to stay on task, but I can't make myself pull away from him. His warmth is too inviting, and his scent is light and crisp, like clean sheets fresh from the dryer and a surprising hint of something sharp, like bergamot.

I clear my throat. "Well, uh, we need signs. I don't suppose you'd be willing to help with that?" I suggest.

His smile changes from playful to thoughtful. It's a quiet moment until he responds. "Sure. I'll give it my best shot. What vibe are we going for?"

Surprisingly, for the next twenty minutes, we have a natural and easy conversation while brainstorming our ideas for the signage for the Maple Falls Harvest Feast. We come up with some pretty good stuff and a list of supplies we'll need to make it happen.

"I'll get the supplies tomorrow, and then you can–"

"No, no," Travis says, hopping down from the barstool and pulling mine out. "We're going shopping together, right now."

He spins my stool around until I'm facing him, his hands light but confident on my knees.

"But—"

"You don't have to work today, right?" he asks.

I shake my head.

"You don't have other plans?"

I shake my head again.

"Then it's settled," he says with a boyish grin. He leans forward until our faces are less than a foot apart.

"It's settled," I whisper in agreement.

The way he's looking at me, the way he insists we spend time together... I can't be mistaken, right? I think he wants... me.

"Do you want to drive or should I?" I ask.

"What kind of trunk space do you have?" he asks.

"Plenty," I reply. "I'll show you."

I change into a pair of my little sneaker/ballet-flat combo shoes and grab a few canvas bags for the shopping. Travis follows me out to my little one-car garage and grasps my shoulders when he sees my car.

"Cally, you've got to be kidding me! How did I not know you drove a car that's almost as beautiful as you are?"

I sputter out a laugh at the strange but welcome comment. "I walk a lot," I tell him.

"Why?" he asks, releasing me and moving over to my old convertible and gingerly running his fingertips over the fender. "A 1950s Dodge Coronet? How did you—"

Apparently, Travis is a car guy. I never would have guessed that. Somehow, it hasn't come up in our conversation so far, though I suppose there is still a lot we have to learn about each other. If we keep wanting to learn about each other.

"My grandpa left it to me when he passed. My brother was so angry," I tell him, crossing my arms.

Travis just stares at it with bewildered eyes and an open mouth.

"You want to drive it?" I ask. "It probably needs some exercise."

"You're kidding, right?" he asks, dropping his hand from the car and coming back over to me. "You trust me that much?"

"I do owe you one," I tease, remembering our little banter that first night in the restaurant.

"Careful, or I'm going to fall for you," he says, growing a little bit serious. He reaches up and gently hooks a finger under my chin.

It's too much. I pull my chin away and grab my keys out of my bag. "Don't tease me."

I press the keys into his hand and climb in the passenger side, reaching over to push on the garage door opener. Travis is absolutely giddy when the engine roars to life.

"Can we ride with the top down?" His eyes are pleading.

"Isn't it a bit cold for that?"

A little bit of light dies out behind those green orbs, and I can't have that. I'm too weak. I reach over and press the button to let the top down.

"At least it's a sunny day," I mutter, taking the scarf from around my neck and tying it over my hair.

He has to step out to move his rental car out onto the street, but he's back quickly, and soon we're on our way.

We take the long way around town, stopping at a few different places to get decorations and art supplies for our plans. It's actually really nice and natural, and we both ease back into our usual teasing. And he's still looking at me like I'm the only woman in the world.

And I've gone back to feeling like I'm helplessly falling head over heels for him.

We stop for a couple of specialty fall drinks at a local coffeeshop just across the street from my parents' restaurant. Travis gets a maple pecan latte, stating that he might be bouncing off the walls later. I get a classic caramel apple spice latte. On the way back to the car, my mom sees me and gives me a wide-eyed look before a smile creeps over her face. She flashes a thumbs up. I'm afraid Travis is going to see her, so I take hold of his jacket sleeve and pull him along faster.

Maybe it's just an excuse to drive a little more, but he suggests that we go to his parents' place to work since they have a spare room with lots of working space, not to mention some of his old art supplies. I'm a little nervous to run into his parents, but I think this could be one of those golden opportunities to find out more about him.

The Thatcher house is nice and well kept. It's decorated in a traditional aesthetic, with lots of family pictures and artwork, mostly landscapes, hanging on the walls. We grab all the shopping bags, and Travis takes my hand and leads me to the spare room. It seems like a kind of hobby space with a big table, easels, an overflowing bookshelf, and some home gym equipment.

We quickly find our groove and get to work. He prepares the signs, and I focus on my menu some more, making sure I'll have all the ingredients I'll need.

"Travis?" a woman's voice calls out from down the hall. "Are you here?"

He gets up and sticks his head out of the door. "Yeah, it's me."

It's got to be his mom. Her voice is getting closer. "Whose car is that? Your dad's trying to take pictures of it—"

Travis looks back at me and wiggles, juts his chin, and gives what seems to be a silent sigh to prepare to meet his mother. His smile is reassuring. Timidly, I get up and stand close beside him.

"Oh!" Travis's mom exclaims upon seeing me. "You have a friend here?"

Travis nods and gestures back to me. "This is Cally," he says, gleaming.

His mom seems surprised, but she takes in the look on his face and seems to ease up a little and offers me her hand. "I'm Elizabeth, Travis's mom."

"It's nice to meet you," I say, bowing my head down a little and taking her hand.

"What are you two up to?" she asks.

Just then, the man I assume to be Travis's dad comes around the corner, breathless. "Is that your car, young lady?" he asks.

I stifle a chuckle. This must be a trait he shares with his dad. I'm happy to see it. "Yes, it is."

"I hope you don't mind if I took a couple of pictures. That thing's a beaut!"

"Dad, really?" Travis mutters.

I place my hand on his back and smile at his dad. "It's perfectly fine, Mr. Thatcher."

His parents hang around for a couple of minutes, and we explain to them what we're doing. His mom seems surprised that Travis has surrounded himself with art supplies. Overall, his parents are perfectly nice, just like all the residents of our lovely Maple Falls.

They leave us a short time later, and we head back to the table, where we sit a little closer this time. Travis is cutting something out, and I'm watching him. Suddenly, I have the urge to know... at least one thing.

"Travis?" I ask.

"Hmm?" He's still focused on cutting the perfect line, the tip of his tongue barely peeking out between his lips.

"Travis," I say again. I tug on the fabric of his shirt hanging around his midsection.

He looks over at me, slow and steady. His attention is now one hundred percent mine.

"When are you... going back to Chicago?" I sputter out the words.

His face is unchanged, peacefully gazing upon me. "I'm thinking of... not doing that."

I grip his shirt a little tighter. "You mean... just stay here? Quit your existing life... cold turkey?"

I can't help a slight grin at her choice of phrases, but my question is a serious one. "What do you think?" he asks, his voice gentle and low.

Honestly, it makes me want to cry with relief, but that feels a little too emotional and irrational. "Well, I for one feel like this town has a lot going for it."

Travis laughs lightly and leans over to rest his forehead against mine. "I agree," he whispers. "And isn't the leftover turkey the best part of Thanksgiving?"

CHAPTER 18

THE MAPLE FALLS HARVEST FEAST IS TOMORROW, AND IT'S TIME TO get cooking. I'm grateful that Cally let me tag along, but I have no idea what I'm doing.

"I'm not sure how much you're expecting from me," I mutter, sneaking up behind Cally, who's flipping through her clipboard of recipes. I place my hands on the counter on either side of her.

I hear her breath hitch. "Travis," she growls. Really, she growls at me like an angry cat. "We have work to do!" It's pretty adorable, actually, but I get the message and back away.

"Got it," I say. "Business only. For now."

The restaurant is closed today in preparation for the event, so it's just the two of us. I thought maybe Cally's family, or at least her dad, would be here, but apparently her parents are enjoying a rare day off.

This is actually the first time in a few days that Cally and I have gotten to hang out together since the day we drove around in her super cool car and spent hours talking and working on the signage for the Thanksgiving event. That day, she asked me if I was going back to Chicago, and I basically told her I don't think I want to.

We haven't talked about it since then, and I don't want to, not right now anyway. I want to focus on her.

"Did you ever go to this event before?" Cally asks, choosing a couple of recipes and hanging them up for easy and hands-free reading.

I want to be helpful to her, so I keep studying the layout of the kitchen, opening the cabinets and drawers so I know where to find the tools and ingredients we'll need. "Not for several years," I admit. "After graduating, I just came over for short trips during the holidays. I wasn't here long enough to attend both the town's Thanksgiving and my family's Thanksgiving."

Cally hums. "Well, it's gotten really huge. People come from all over now. It's almost as big as the Fall Leaves Festival."

I study Cally for a moment. She's a mix of excitement and focus. It's like I can see her body literally jittering. Dang, every time I see her, she gets even more adorable. She's all business today, committed to spending hours in the kitchen, and her 'all-business' work attire suits her. She's wearing a pair of green baggy overalls with a multi-color striped, long sleeve sweater underneath. Her sleeves are pushed up to her elbows. She's also wearing a pair of white sneakers, and her hair is in what she explained are called 'space buns.' For the finishing touch, she's tied a little scarf around her head to keep the little flyaways out of her face.

"You're staring at me again," she says, with a glaring side eye.

Even though there's no way to misinterpret my feelings for her at this point, she is fighting me. Ever since we met up this morning, she's been meeting every aspect of my affection with feisty feigned reprove. Touch her hand? She tells me not to tease her. Stare at her beautiful face longingly? She tells me to stop staring. Tell her she's the most beautiful woman I've ever seen in person or on a screen? She tells me to stop trying so hard.

But behind every glare and scowl, I know she's fighting a smile. It just makes me want to tease her more.

"Don't forget your apron!" I say. "You've been wearing the patchwork one lately, right?"

"Oh, yeah, thanks," she says.

I grab the apron from the hook near the door. She reaches toward me to take it, but I evade her grasp. "I've got it," I tell her, standing behind her and reaching my arms around her waist to situate the apron. "I'm going to be the best assistant ever."

I quickly tie the apron strings into a little bow and plant a quick kiss on Cally's cheek.

When I step away she's frozen. I count to ten. She still doesn't move. Ten more seconds….

I spin her around by the shoulders. She's blushing bright red. Then she stares up at me fiercely. "A good assistant wouldn't distract me!"

I can't help but chuckle. "Fine, fine. I'm one hundred percent serious. Starting now. No more teasing."

She huffs to cover her amusement, but I think I can read her well enough by now to know she's not truly irritated.

We're starting with the desserts since they keep and reheat better. Next, will be the sides, and tomorrow we'll come in early to cook the main dish. At first, Cally does everything. She talks me through the recipe for a sweet and tangy cream pie, explaining her technique and what ingredients serve which purpose. I'll have to suggest the whole cookbook idea again later.

Soon enough, I'm peaking over her shoulder, reading ahead in the recipe and anticipating her needs. One cup of flour? No problem. I grab the measuring cup and the flour. Cream cheese? I know where that is! Fresh lemon juice? I've recently been complimented on my ability to use a manual juicer.

Really, we work well together. At first, she insisted on doing everything herself, but as we get into the second dessert, she's easing up. Watching her in the kitchen is like watching a bee expertly buzzing around the garden, knowing precisely which flowers to visit, and returning back to its hive.

When I notice that the dishes are starting to stack up, I get my hands in the sink and wash them. It's kind of fun. I've never really done anything like this before. There's a goal to be met, and I'm having a good time getting to it. I don't feel pressured to be perfect or to have a certain outcome. Even Cally doesn't seem too worried. If she questions the taste, she gives me a small bite, and I tell her how delicious it is. End of concern.

I can't help but think that it feels like we're made to do this together. We're in perfect sync. On her own, Cally is incredible, but I love feeling how we work side by side.

We're almost finished for the night. Cally is in the middle of a delicious smelling dish of scalloped potato stacks. She says they're like fancy scalloped potatoes that are easy to share considering the large event with so many people to feed.

I watch her expertly chop the potatoes that I previously washed and peeled—well, helped peel. She tosses them in various types of seasoning that I don't know the names of. The smell is fragrant, though. She piles them in a muffin tin and spoons a mixture of cream over them before garnishing them with rosemary and cheese.

"Man, I wanna do that," I say, sulking a little.

Cally giggles. "Well, maybe you can help cook for your family Thanksgiving. Mashed potatoes are a good starter dish."

The suggestion sounds perfect. "Do you want to?" I ask, leaning against the counter, close to her.

"Do I want to what?" she asks, pausing from her task and looking over her shoulder at me.

There's a little speck of something on her cheek, probably a remnant of some seasoning. I brush it off with my thumb, and while I'm at it, because it's irresistible not to touch her all that I can, I smooth back a couple of the hairs peeking out from under her scarf.

She's looking from one of my eyes to the other like she can't decide which one to land on. "Do what?" she mutters.

"Spend Thanksgiving together." It's seamless. "You know, mashed potatoes."

She tucks her lips in, suddenly a little unsure. "What about your family? You should really be with them, you know, especially because of your aunt's situation and all. And you said you missed last year."

I let my hand fall. Her declination is polite, but it still stings. She does have a point, but I want to spend more time with her. Maybe she's not ready for that kind of commitment yet. "Right."

"Well," she says quickly on a sigh, "it's probably high time for a break. Yeah? Let's leave this here, and I'll come back later to check that the bread is rising properly."

She spins around and carries the rest of the potatoes, now soaking in water, to the back to the fridge to be cooked later.

I capture her hand as she's rushing by. It seems like she's avoiding my eyes all of a sudden. "Cally," I say. I'm sure I've never said her name so gravely before. But something in her demeanor has me worried. Am I misreading something?

"You mean, we will come back later, right?" For some reason, my heart is pounding in my chest.

"Oh, yeah. Sure," she responds. She starts to twist away. "You can come, too. Sure."

This isn't right.

"Cally," I say again. "What's wrong?"

She sucks in a deep breath. Just when I think she's going to release it, she doesn't. Her chest stays slightly puffed. She's staring down at the ground, the hand I'm holding flexing and unflexing.

"It's a little weird, right?" she finally says after too long.

"What?"

"It's just, do you mean it?" she asks, braving a look up at me. "Thanksgiving together already? We've only gone on one date. It's only been a couple of weeks. And I know you said you were thinking of not going back to Chicago and all, but that's a pretty big decision. it seems like you were eager to get out of here back then. At first, you were talking about being CEO. Is that something you really want to abandon?"

I stare at her incredulously. Has she really been thinking all of this the whole time?

"Have I not been clear enough with you?" I ask, sliding my fingers around her small palm.

"I mean," she starts, eyes back on the floor again, "it seems like I know what you feel, but then once in a while I have these thoughts that make me doubt why you like me. All of the things you say you like about me are the very things everyone else judges me for."

Oh. I think I kind of understand where she's coming from.

"Cally," I say a little more softly. "If other people judge you, or don't like you for all the reasons I like you, then they're all crazy. You are an original—unique, beautiful, creative. You have such a big heart. But really, I don't believe it."

"Don't believe what?" she whispers, looking a little hurt.

I smile and take her face in my hands. "I don't think people see you the way you think they do. Sure, maybe there's someone once in a while who gets you wrong, but that happens to all of us. I think people love you. I've seen it–at your booth, in this restaurant, on the street. I just pray one day you can see it, too."

She gulps and nods.

I step behind her to untie her apron and hang it back on its hook. We get in my car and grab some takeout Chinese before heading back to her place to rest, where she pops in a silly rom-com and we chat about little things. The vibe between us is different than before but still comfortable. I can tell she keeps getting sucked into her own thoughts. But if I've learned anything from being my mother's keeper all these years, it's that I can't force anyone to feel anything. I can't force them to see what I see or to believe it. I just have to affirm them and support them until they do.

A couple of hours later, it's time to go check on the bread.

"Have you ever been thrifting before?" she asks me out of the blue as we pull into a parking spot outside the Maple Falls Cafe.

"Maybe we can add—" My words fall short as I look past the nose of the car. "Uh, Cally...."

She follows my gaze outside the car, and her jaw goes slack at the smashed in windows of her parents' restaurant, the glass splattered all across the pavement.

She puts her hand on the handle to get out, but I stop her.

CHAPTER 19

"We should call the police first," Travis tells me.

"Wh-what is this? What happened?" I sputter, covering my mouth with both hands.

He already has his phone out. "Wait here," he says to me. "I'm going to check it out, okay?"

"W—wait." Is it safe? It looks dangerous with the broken glass everywhere. He walks through the smashed-in door with his cell-phone pressed up against his ear. My heart hammers in my chest.

How can I wait here when he's going in there? What if the intruder is still there? I jet out of the car and run after him. I step over the shards of glass from the front door and spot him approaching the kitchen. He hears me coming and frowns back at me but doesn't tell me to leave as I take his hand.

"I don't think there's anyone here now," he says both to me and the police on the phone as we step through the swinging door.

I'm about to drop his hand at the same time he's clutching mine. The kitchen is an absolute wreck. The fridge is swung wide open with everything inside strewn across the floor. There are bits of food scattered everywhere, and every container has been poured out onto the tile in a heap. The bread that was rising on the counter has literally been pummeled.

"Everything is destroyed," I squeak out, my breath nearly caught in my throat.

Travis finishes the call with the police, and I get my parents on the phone. My dad answers and tells my mom to get out of bed and get dressed. The police arrive, and then Mom and Dad pull up. We have to answer a bunch of questions and step out of the restaurant while they take photos and collect whatever evidence may have been left behind. It's almost midnight by the time they leave, and we're permitted to reenter.

My mom wraps me up in a hug, cradling my head in the crook of her elbow. Travis watches me closely while he helps my dad sift through what's left.

"What am I going to do, Mom?" I mutter into her shoulder. She smells like the lotion she puts on every night, like cocoa butter and a hint of lemon. "There's no way I can make all of this food again. I was so excited...."

"Oh, honey," she croons. "I'm so sorry. I know you were looking forward to this event. You always are. But we still have our family Thanksgiving to cook for. We can salvage some ingredients and make some of the simpler recipes."

"No," I say quietly, stepping out of her embrace. Frustration bubbles up inside as I realize how big of a missed opportunity this truly will be. "I wanted to share these with everyone. That way, I'll know what works and what people like. It's my only chance to add my own creativity to the menu."

Mom looks surprised, and she throws a glance over my shoulder, probably at my dad. Within seconds, Travis rushes over to my side.

"I'll help you," he says earnestly. "Whatever you need, however long it takes. I'll even buy the replacement groceries."

"Hang on," Mom says. She pats my shoulder on her way over to my father. Their conversation is hushed.

"Cally," Travis murmurs, placing a hand on each of my shoulders and looking me in the eyes. "It'll be okay. We can make it work. It's obviously not ideal, but I don't want you to miss out on this opportunity either. I know how hard you've been working toward it."

I gesture weakly to the mess that is the kitchen. "But it's—"

"It's a disaster," he finishes for me, a small, encouraging smile tugging at the corners of his mouth. "But we are going to fix it."

I'm not convinced. It seems like too big of a task. We've already put in so many hours of work, and the feast is tomorrow. "We'd have to spend the entire night here. All of it."

He seems to take that as a positive reaction, and his smile grows a bit more. "Let's start with a list, yeah?"

I'm about to respond when my parents both come over. This certainly wasn't the way I wanted Travis to meet my parents. I haven't even properly introduced them amid all the chaos. But Travis is standing next to me like the confident man he is, and I couldn't be more proud.

"I know this is your thing, and I want to help," Dad begins. "But I think for the sake of your purpose for this year's meal, I shouldn't be part of the cooking process. Why don't you and your friend go into the city and hit the twenty-four-hour grocery store? Your mom and I will stay here and get all this cleaned up so you can start cooking as soon as you get back. Okay?"

The cleanup will be immense, but if I don't have to worry about that, I can focus on the cooking, and if we stay all night, we should get it done.

For some reason, my dad telling me he doesn't want to be involved in the cooking fills me with relief. It's not that I don't want him to help, but I'd be afraid he'd end up taking over and making his usual recipes again. Maybe he knows that, too. This is his way of being supportive.

Dad gives me the keys to the van we usually reserve for catering. Travis drives while I make a list of all the ingredients we'll need to replace. My brain feels blurry and bogged down but also like it's in high gear. It's try or die.

The twenty-four-hour grocery store doesn't have every single ingredient I'll need, but I'm able to get some reasonable replacements so I can make the menu I'd intended. Travis runs along beside me between the aisles, grabbing each of the items on my list. For a moment, when he's carrying over an armload of cream cheese, milk, whipping cream, and butter, I'm sort of mesmerized by him. He's so constant, dependable. And he truly understands how important it is to me to do this.

As he's loading things into the cart, I put my arm on his and lift on my tiptoes up to give him a quick peck on the cheek. He freezes, but I can tell by the brightness of his green eyes that he's mostly amazed.

"Thank you," I tell him.

He blinks a couple of times. "Yeah."

Then, it's back to the shopping. We wrap up our unanticipated grocery trip. He pays for everything, impervious to my dissuasion against it. Together, we map out a game plan on the drive back.

When we arrive, the place is fairly spotless. The gaping holes in the glass door are covered with plywood, and the lock is fixed. At least we'll be safe while we cook. I'm thankful the police didn't see the need to mark the whole area off with crime tape for an extended period of time.

My parents help us unload the groceries, but then my parents bow out. I'm torn between wanting more hands on deck and more autonomy.

"It's a good thing I'm a fast learner," Travis says, readying himself to take on the peeling of potatoes and the chopping of various veggies.

I start with the bread this time. "Someone literally punched my dough," I growl. "How passive aggressive can you be?"

Travis frowns. "Who would have done something like this? And why? They didn't even take anything. They could have raided the register with access to the restaurant like this, but they didn't even touch it."

While I'm measuring out the flour for the bread, I'm back in my element, so I can think clearly again. My mind finally loops back into its usual processing ability, and something occurs to me. "I think this was an attack on me."

Travis stops his chopping. "What? But why?"

I shrug. "I don't know why. But if it was a real burglary, they would have taken stuff. If it was an attack on my parents, they would have trashed the booths and turned over the tables or something, but they only hit the kitchen, and only after I—we—spent an entire day in here working."

"That's… hard to believe," Travis says.

He's not saying I'm wrong. It is weird. Crime isn't usually a problem in Maple Falls. In fact, I can't even remember the last time something like this happened. After a brief moment of silence, Travis gets back to his duties as my assistant. "Maybe the police will find something."

I sigh. "Yeah. Let's just focus on the food for now."

Hours later, when the dull light of dawn starts to spread on the horizon, Travis and I make it to a stopping point. We're running on whatever sleep we got from the night before… that and pure determination.

I lean against the counter with my eyes half closed. Travis rubs my arm. "Cally, why don't you get some rest?"

I shake my head. "What if someone comes back?"

"It's almost daylight. I don't think anyone is going to try anything else. Plus, there are two cars out front now, and the police said they'd circle the block all night."

I split my eyes open just enough to catch sight of his handsome face, which is a bit blurry in my exhaustion. "I can't go home," I say. "I have to put stuff in the oven soon."

"I know," he says. His voice is pure and gentle. "Why don't you take a rest here? You can lie down in one of those booths and use my coat for a blanket. It'll be warmer in here with the oven going, too."

I hum in agreement. Twenty minutes of shut eye does sound pretty heavenly about now. "What about you?" I mumble. The thought of sleep has caused me to slur my words. In fact, I might be half asleep right now.

"I'll stay here and watch everything," he tells me, patting my hair. "I'll keep an eye out, and when a timer goes off, I'll take whatever it is out of the oven."

"You should sleep, too," I mutter as he guides me toward a booth.

He chuckles softly. I like the sound when it's so close to me. "I'll see what I can do."

I'm pretty sure I'm dozing before he finishes his sentence.

CHAPTER 20

When the cooking is done, I drop Cally off at her house and then return to my parents' so we can freshen up quickly. Between the two of us, we managed to get four hours of sleep combined. I tossed and turned in the booth where I'd finally rested. Even my exhaustion wasn't enough to ignore the small, cramped space and the cold coming in through parts of the broken window, even though her dad had boarded them up.

With Jeremiah and Casey's help, my signs and banners were dispersed around town a couple of days ago, and I pass by one on my way to my parents' house. It feels pretty good to use my creative energy for once, and it's amazing to see my signs out in the wild, even though I didn't use my usual medium to create them.

According to Cally, the Maple Falls Harvest Feast is going to be bigger than it's ever been this year. There are all kinds of events around town, sort of a traveling buffet, and Maple Falls Cafe is one of the most popular stops. I might have known this if I hadn't totally checked out of Maple Falls as soon as I left for college. I have to admit, though, it's fun to see the town so excited.

"Travis," my mother says from the breakfast nook as I walk in the door. "Are you just getting home? I didn't hear you last night."

She must realize that I wasn't out doing anything nefarious, because when she gets a good look at me, she sets her coffee down and springs up from the table.

"Yeah." I laugh half-heartedly. "It was a long night."

"What on earth happened? You look like you haven't slept in three days. And what's all over your shirt?" She picks at my Henley with a disgusted look on her face.

"I helped Cally make a Thanksgiving feast. Twice."

She crosses her arms and pinches her eyebrows together. "Why twice?"

I recount the story of our initial kitchen conquering and how, when we left for all of an hour and a half, we came back to find it all destroyed.

"We've been working on the second round since midnight," I tell her. "Cally's parents are there now, getting the glass in the door replaced and cleaning up some more."

My mom looks incredulous. "My boy," she says with a sigh. "I've never seen you so dedicated to something. And even though you look like you've gone through a war with a hoard of bakers, I can see that you're enjoying it. There's a brightness in your eyes that wasn't there when you first got here."

I loop my arm around my mom's shoulders and give her a gentle kiss on top of her head. Whatever she's been feeling for the last couple of weeks, it seems like she's getting over it. I make a mental note to talk to her a bit later when I'm refreshed and refueled.

I pick up Cally and swing her through a drive-thru since I know full-well neither of us has had had a proper meal in fourteen hours, even though we've been in a kitchen cooking for all that time. We tasted a few of the dishes to make sure they were right, but that hardly counts. On the way, Cally cheers every time she sees one of the signs we made.

"You did such a good job!" she tells me between bites of her breakfast burrito. "If they weren't already interested in the food, people surely would come to see who made such beautiful signs."

I think most of what she's saying is exaggerated from her exhaustion, but I accept it. "I'm glad I was able to help in whatever way I could." I take a sip of my drink, and I'm grateful for the shot of caffeine and sugar that comes with it.

"I think you've more than proved yourself," she says. "You're one step closer to making mashed potatoes on your own, anyway."

I can't help but chuckle. I'm not so sure about that.

As we're driving through the town, I spot so many cars with different license plates: Ohio, Michigan, New York, even one from as far away as South Carolina. This truly must be quite an experience for people to drive hundreds of miles to get here today. No wonder we made so much food.

Cally scrambles out of the car when she sees the time. "I need to get some stuff in the oven!" she shouts.

I laugh and chase after her. We've been together for almost two entire days now. Our only time apart was when we showered and changed clothes this morning.

Even so, I still can't get enough of her. I even love the way she orders me around in the kitchen. I love the surprised, but grateful, look on her face as I've tried to anticipate each of her requests. I'm intrigued by her unique outfits and the way she does her hair.

I also can't get enough of her smile, her laugh, and even her teasing. I especially love it when she blushes. And right now, I'm so happy, so content, to be with her as she flits around the restaurant taking orders and delivering delicious meals to customer after customer.

I've had the opportunity now to properly meet Mr. and Mrs. Stein, David and Sheila. They're both lovely people. Sheila assigned me the role of helping seat customers and ringing them up.

"Your pretty face will draw people in who don't already have a reservation," Cally adds with a wink.

"I think the smell alone is enough to tempt anyone to walk through the door," I reply.

For about three hours, Sheila and I man the front, greeting hungry customers and sending off deliriously full ones. Around 2:00, David comes up front and lets us know that everything is gone.

"Everything?" Sheila shrieks.

He laughs sheepishly, looking proud but afraid to say it out loud. "Yes, every last bit."

Then the realization hits me. "Wait, so I don't even get to try any of it?"

David looks at me with a friendly smile. I still haven't talked to him much, but I like him. I can tell he's a kind man who takes his work seriously. "I think some of these items might have to be seasonal, if not permanent additions to the menu," he says. "So, Travis, you can come in and eat them whenever you want."

Cally pops around him just then. "Do you mean that?" she asks, looking genuinely amazed. "Can I add some of my dishes to your menu?"

He twists around and wraps his daughter up in a big bear hug. "It'll be our menu, honey," he says. "I'm sorry I've been resisting for so long. I know how hard you work and how talented you are, but I guess I just didn't want to take the risk. But you're so creative, honey, and it's clear that everyone loves all the dishes you created."

Cally's eyes overflow as she hugs him back. A swell of happiness and pride rises in my chest, too. This is such a big step for her as she works toward inheriting this place.

At the end of the day, despite being exhausted, Cally and I both are elated. She's giddy with the number of compliments that she's received from customers and totally thrilled that her dad is finally letting her add her own stuff to the menu.

"Do you wanna try some more cooking?" she asks me with a witty smile.

I let out a tired chuckle. "Really? You're thinking about cooking right now?"

She presses her lips together in an unapologetic smile. "Well, I'm gonna go home and test out at least one new recipe. If you wanna miss out on that, then that's on you."

She's so amazing. How can I resist? Not to mention that I'm also still buzzing with energy despite the lack of sleep. I caught some compliments about the 'eye-catching' and 'uniquely artistic' signs on the wind. It's great to hear that people appreciate my art, so I want to celebrate, too.

We crawl like overzealous slugs into my rental car, which I am actually getting quite tired of. Cally lets out an extended groan and tosses the seat back.

"Are you sure you have the energy to make dinner?" I ask her.

She lulls her head to the side to face me. "Aren't you starving for something other than fast food?" she says.

It's true. We've had takeout for breakfast, for lunch, and even before we started cooking yesterday, despite making so many dishes from scratch for others. "You're right, of course. What will it be?"

"Listen," she starts, sitting up in the seat and looking at me seriously, "I know you have the taste of a sixteen-year-old, so how do you feel about a fancy pizza?"

I snort. It's not the first time she's teased me, especially since the French restaurant. She likes to comment about my food choices. I'll admit that I never made it a priority to cook when I went away to college. I ate a lot of takeout and made a lot of spaghetti and mac and cheese. It was just… easier.

"Just how fancy is this pizza?" I ask, narrowing my eyes.

"Maple bacon and caramelized onion, with real mozzarella."

I put the car in drive and back out. "Bacon? I'm totally in."

Cally giggles and tosses herself back into the reclined seat again.

We get to her house, and Cally gets to cooking while I go back to being her assistant, doing whatever I can to help. While the pizza bakes, my mind wanders. Maybe it's my exhaustion, but things in my past are suddenly clear.

When I graduated from high school, I had tunnel vision. I wanted to get away from my parents, not because I didn't love them, but because I felt like I was frequently used as an emotional barricade between them. They failed to communicate their issues and let grudges build up inside them.

My mom's answer was to use me as her shield and her safety blanket. It was exhausting sometimes. My dad's answer was to go to work. I felt like I was doing my father's job tending to my mother's emotions, and it didn't leave much room for me to process my own. I think I resented them both for a long time because of it. I resisted coming home because I didn't want to get sucked back into it. My mom still called me sometimes when she was upset with my dad, while I rarely heard from my dad.

Also, I wanted to get away from this town. I was good at a lot of different activities, and throughout most of middle school and high school, I wanted to impress everyone. I entered art contests, volunteered, put in extra time for football and basketball, and studied hard so I could be at the top of my class. Looking back, it started out as an opportunity for recognition. I felt so hidden at home, so I wanted to shine everywhere else. But I wore out before high school ended. It felt like I'd started living under a microscope, and I needed space.

I switched gears but over-corrected. I withdrew too much from Maple Falls and put up walls between my family and me. I zeroed in on my job as if it were the most important thing in the world. I wanted to prove something to myself, that I could do amazing things for me and not because someone else expected me to. But all the while, I was actually losing sight of myself.

Since being back in Maple Falls, since meeting Cally, since almost losing Aunt Ine… I've remembered what's important. A spark has lit in me, and I don't want to let it out ever again.

I'm rethinking everything. Small towns aren't so bad. In fact, there's something special about them—this one in particular. I miss having close friends. I want to sit in nature with my aunt and draw what I see.

Maybe passions are different from jobs. Sometimes they line up, but sometimes they stand alone. I don't need to limit myself to a job or a passion, even if they don't end up being the same thing. And maybe success is possible regardless of which activities I choose to give more of my time to.

Cally lets me have the first bite of the pizza. I sink my teeth into it, and flavor explodes over my tongue. "This is so freaking good," I mutter, shoving another big bite into my mouth. "You only made one?"

She hits me playfully on the shoulder and grabs a slice for herself. "We'll make it side by side next time and see who makes the best one."

"Seems unfair," I say with my mouth full.

She shrugs with a smug smile and chews her pizza, taking a moment to enjoy the cheese and the sweet tang of the bacon. "Would it be crazy to put little sweet potato chunks on here?" she asks.

I shrug, though it does sound good.

We chat for a few minutes over the shared pizza. I tell her a little bit about my relationship with my parents and what drove me to want to leave home after high school.

"I think I was just being dramatic," I admit.

Cally shakes her head. "Don't minimize yourself or your feelings, Travis. I think that sort of environment would wear anyone down."

I nod and ask her if she wants the last slice. She declines, so I finish it off. "I think it's time for both of us to get some rest," I tell her.

She sighs but agrees and walks me to the front door.

"The sooner you go to bed, the sooner you get to see me tomorrow," I whisper close to her ear.

Cally crosses her arms. "Oh? Am I seeing you tomorrow? It's awfully brave of you to assume that."

I break into a toothy grin and step back to see her also fighting a brilliant smile. "So tomorrow then," I say without question.

She feigns indifference. "I suppose I wouldn't mind that."

When I get back to my parents' house, I realize I have a lot of work emails piling up. I hunker down at my desk and do what I can to respond to Mr. Erkin's questions about my whereabouts and the presentation that's still lingering somewhere out of his reach, done but undelivered.

I guess it's time for a phone call after all. There are a lot of things I could quit cold turkey, but Cally Stein isn't one of them.

CHAPTER 21

CALLY

MY FAVORITE HOLIDAY HAS FINALLY COME! IT'S THANKSGIVING!

Even though I work at a restaurant with my father, Thanksgiving and Christmas are the only two holidays where everyone in the house cooks together. My dad might be the chef at Maple Falls Cafe, but my mom makes a pretty mean turkey! The thing is, we have a pretty big family, so it's an all-hands-on-deck kind of situation.

Mom, Dad, and I share the kitchen for the first few hours of the day. Each of us chooses a main course and a side. Besides that, it's my turn to make dessert this year. I make some pastries in honor of Travis since he's spending the holiday with his parents and his aunt. My siblings will each provide a side, usually a kid-friendly one, and probably some cookies.

My parents' home is filled with the aromas of baking turkey, rosemary, crispy potatoes, well-seasoned veggies, cranberries, baking apples, and all sorts of spices. It smells like heaven!

"Why don't you work on a couple of seasonal dishes that we can introduce for the Christmas season?" my dad suddenly suggests, bumping into my side. "And maybe we can sit down later and talk about a couple of additions to the menu."

I don't want to question it anymore or be overly polite and ask my dad if he's sure. I never thought he'd allow me to do this, at least not until the restaurant was mine some day, and even then, he'd probably have some kind of clause in there where I'd have to promise not to make changes to most or all of the dishes. But now's my chance, and I'm jumping in headfirst!

"I have so many ideas that would suit the vibe of the cafe," I tell him excitedly. "What if we introduced a couple of pizza options?! They'd be kind of elevated and special but also normal enough for our laid-back setting. Oh, and I have a few ideas for new soups. Maybe that can be one of the seasonal dishes. People love a good soup, and I think it'd pair well with lots of the items we already have on the menu."

My dad chuckles. It's a low, gruff sound that comes from deep within him. He places a hand on my shoulder and gives it a squeeze. "I'd love to hear all about it, Cal," he says, "but your squash is gonna burn...."

I jerk back into action. Burning a delicious dish like stuffed butternut squash is a crime!

Dad goes outside to the smoker, where he's been working on his meaty main dish, brisket. Mom's got the turkey in the oven, and I'm about to start my dish on the stove: rosemary and apple cider chicken.

"You always add that little extra zing, don't you?" Mom teases as I'm piling my ingredients on the counter. "Not just plain old baked chicken, but rosemary apple cider chicken!" Every syllable at the end of her sentence gets a little extra flourish.

I smile down at the apples and start to cut them. My smile fades just a little. I'm happy to be here cooking with my family, but last weekend gave me the opportunity to cook alongside Travis, and it was absolutely magical. I wish he were here to tease me, too.

My mom must catch the shift in my mood because she sidles up next to me and rests her head on my shoulder. She lets out a dreamy sigh. "If only that strapping young man were here. Am I right? He's such a gentleman. And he's quite funny, too."

"Yes, Mom," I admit. "He really is."

Mom clears her throat and peeks up at me under her eyelashes. "So… are you two dating or…?"

I give a little shrug, and her head bobs up and down with the motion, but she keeps it on my shoulder. "I don't know," I reply. "I mean, he said he was thinking about not going back to Chicago, but I don't know. If he does, then—"

My heart twists at the thought. Then, I would really hate it.

Mom straightens up and grabs a spring of rosemary to strip. "Oh, honey, I can tell you like him a lot. And I'm sure he likes you, too."

"I know," I mutter. "But that isn't always enough, right? Sometimes life gets in the way, and people want different things. What if it doesn't line up for us? I really want it to." It would be so hard for him to walk away from his life there—especially so suddenly.

Mom tucks a strand of hair behind my ear and looks at me with compassion. "People go where their hearts take them," she says. "Maybe whatever was in his heart that took him to Chicago has changed or worn away. But even if it hasn't, honey, it'll be okay. It'll be tough, but we'll all be here for you."

Over the last few weeks, I've gotten to know Travis and his heart. He sort of wears it on his sleeve. When we cooked together, we did everything in sync. And when we were faced with an impossible problem, he rolled up his sleeves and made sure that I didn't give up and that everything came together for the Maple Falls Harvest Feast. Then, of course, there's the way he looks at me, the way his eyes study me like he's trying to commit every tiny detail to memory. I've noticed it since the beginning.

Maybe he will go back to his busy life in Chicago in the end, but I don't think his heart will be satisfied there. Still, I hope he doesn't go back at all. I hope he realizes that he can do what he loves here and that here, he can truly relax and slow down, like the rhythm of nature in Maple Falls that inspired him so much when he was younger.

The front door opens, and in rush my nieces and nephews. My

oldest brother, Damon, comes straight to the kitchen like a blood-hound trained on Thanksgiving turkey. "You look a little somber," he says. He's got the newest addition on his hip, baby Chaea. "What's up with you?"

Jihwan has sprouted at least six inches in the last year, but he still comes running into my arms with his ear-to-ear smile. His mom, Seungri, politely waves from the far side of the kitchen.

"Oh, nothing," Mom answers for me, finally addressing Damon's question. "She's just pining over a boy."

"Mom!" I screech, causing baby Chaea to startle a little. A peck on the head from her daddy, and she's good as new. "It's not—"

I can't bring myself to say it's not like that. But I don't know. It just seems a little early for that. "Don't listen to her," I say instead.

Damon gets that big brother smirk and digs into it. He looks past me to the woman who has betrayed me. "Who is it? Someone from town?"

"Mom," I growl through gritted teeth. I so do not want this entire day to become Pick On Cally Day.

She doesn't pay me any mind, as expected. "Oh, maybe you know him! He's a bit older than Cally. Do you remember Travis Thatcher?"

"The guy who turned down college football and moved some-where across the country?" he asks, his eyes wide.

"Not across the country. Just to Chicago," I mutter. But I've become a side character in their gossip.

Seungri comes to collect her baby and gives me an apologetic smile while leaving me with my brother and mother. They're scheming something. I can tell by the way their little fluffy fox ears are twitching and their all-too-giddy laughter at my expense.

"Aw, artsy nerd meets the jock who always got perfect grades," Damon croons. "It's a classic love story."

"Would you please not toss that word around?" I say over my shoulder. It's, well, it's making me blush, and I don't want them to see it. I am starting to feel like a high schooler all over again.

"You should have seen the way he came to her rescue for the

Harvest Feast. Oh, it was so sweet. Really, you should take some notes, son," Mom says.

I laugh at my brother's expense this time, grateful he's suddenly been pinned under the magnifying glass, even if it's just for a second.

He lets out a confident and dismissive psh and waves his hand. "I'm plenty romantic, right babe?" he calls into the living room.

"Sure, whatever you say, love," Seungri calls back.

Damon quickly turns the conversation back to me, or rather, to Travis. "So, where is this guy? If these two are in love, shouldn't our families be having Thanksgiving together?"

I smack him in the back of the head with a wooden spoon and then toss it in the sink and grab a new one. It's worth having to clean an extra utensil when he yelps.

"Oh, wait, is it like, one-sided?" Damon whispers like he's talking about some awful contractable disease.

Mom sighs. It doesn't sound like an exasperated, melodramatic one this time. I think I feel her staring between my shoulder blades. "Not from the looks of it," she says gently. "But who knows what will happen?"

I think this is about to take a serious turn, and I suddenly want to get out of here. I slide my chicken into the oven. There's barely enough room for it with the giant turkey in there. Everything smells so good. But my heart is squeezing with panic. Why did my mom's voice have to turn so serious when she said that? *Who knows what will happen* sounds so ominous. It leaves me feeling unsettled.

"I'm gonna… go check on Dad," I say. I catch my brother's rare but genuine worried look as I rush past him.

For some reason, I'm nearly in tears by the time I make it outside.

My dad notices instantly. "What's wrong, Cal?" he asks, stepping back from the smoker and wrapping me in a warm hug.

I've run outside without a coat or shoes. It's pretty cold out here. Maybe that's what brought this on. I probably just shocked my body after leaving the heat of the stove and prancing headlong into the forty degree weather outside.

But that's not what I tell Dad. "I think I love him, and I'm afraid he's going to leave," I blurt out through sudden tears.

He responds with a soul-melting squeeze.

Dad is quiet for a minute while I sniffle into his shoulder. Then he pats my hair. "Nobody in their right mind would leave you, honey," he says softly. "And if for some reason he leaves for a while to wrap up his life in Chicago, there's always a chance his heart will bring him back."

I nod and wipe my eyes, but I'm not sure. The thought of saying goodbye to Travis–for good, or even for a little while–has my heart shattering.

CHAPTER 22

"Hey, Mom, can you teach me how to make mashed potatoes?"
I ask.

She's standing in the kitchen next to the oven when I enter the room. Mom's opted for a pot roast this year instead of a turkey because, apparently, she wants to use the oven for a special side, and it's not quite big enough for both. Either that, or she just doesn't want to slave over basting all morning. There's only an hour left until we're due to eat.

Mom scoffs at me like I'm teasing, but when she turns to find me serious, she rolls her eyes and agrees. "I wasn't planning on potatoes, but I do have some. Go grab a few."

"A few like eight?" I ask. I pick up the bag. "How much would this make?"

"Goodness, son," she says with a laugh. "There are just four of us for dinner, and you know your dad isn't big on potatoes. I think three of those big ones will suffice." She takes a couple from the bag, and I put the rest back in the little wooden box where we store them.

"Also, why do we keep them in a box? Don't they need air or something?"

She turns to me again. "Travis, you do realize potatoes grow in the ground, where it's dark."

I shrug. That does make sense, but I don't know much about cooking or food storage, but I want to learn. Cally would probably think I was silly for not knowing where to store potatoes, but at least I know how to peel and chop them.

My dad joins us in the kitchen and stands at the far edge of the counter. He doesn't say anything and just watches us with an amused expression. He'd explained to me earlier that the two of them had talked, he and my mom. She said she felt lonely and forgotten when he went off to work all the time, especially when she was already feeling distressed, and he apologized and promised that he'd be around more often and do better to support her. All of these years of problems finally solved by a single conversation...

"Your son wants to learn to cook all of a sudden," Mom tells Dad.

"Oh, gee. I wonder if it has anything to do with his new friend, the cute little chef," he responds, crossing his arms.

My aunt rolls into the room in her wheelchair pushed by the home nurse, who has been in and out of the house for the last couple of days since they brought her here. Aunt Ine is doing well and is in higher spirits. Her hip is healing slowly but surely, and she's begun physical therapy for her motor function, focusing on her arms while her hip is healing. She's also been working on her speech, and it's already much better. There's still a little lag in what she says sometimes, and when she's tired, her words slur together, but she can communicate just fine.

"Thanks, Carmen," she says to the nurse. "You can park me here and get going. You deserve to take the rest of the day off! I'll put these three to work until I see you again."

She tells Carmen goodbye, and we all tell her to have a happy Thanksgiving as she walks out the door.

We've situated my aunt in our other spare room that's right across the hall from me. There's a hospital bed in there that Aunt Ine says she won't be using for long. I hope she's right.

"Now, what's this about a cute little chef?" she asks, setting her good arm on the armrest of the wheelchair and looking at me expectantly. "You mean Cally, right? Are you two dating now?"

I laugh semi-uncomfortably now that everyone's eyes have zeroed in on me. "Uh, not technically."

"Not technically?! That's absurd!" To my surprise, it's my dad, who seems offended. He crosses his arms at me. "You need to lock her down!

Mom squints her eyes at him. "Honey, I don't think kids use those kinds of words anymore. It sounds a little too… forceful."

I'm still stunned by my dad's unexpected little outburst and his forwardness.

My aunt coughs out a laugh, probably as stunned as me. "To put it more mildly," she says through a smile, "why haven't you made things official with her?"

"I want to," I blurt out. All these eyes on me are making me nervous. Maybe it's the realization that everyone has high expectations for me again. I add, "But, with all the work stuff going on, I couldn't…."

The room is silently waiting for my weak excuse. Do they think I've been stringing her along? Does Cally think I've been stringing her along? It suddenly feels like my stomach is full of rocks.

"Can you just show me how to make mashed potatoes already?" I grumble.

Around 1:30 P.M., my family finally gathers around the table, my dad at one end, my mom at the other, with my aunt and I on either side. She's in her wheelchair still since it's easier than transporting her into a chair while her hip is still tender.

My dad leads us in prayer, and then we dig in. Nobody pressures me about Cally, but they ask a few questions about my plans for Chicago. I skirt around the answers, keeping them vague. I honestly don't know what I'm going to do just yet. Mom and Dad talk about plans for Christmas, and Aunt Ine talks about the kids that she misses since being off work. She wants to go back, but she also wonders if it's time to retire.

My mom and I take turns helping Aunt Ine cut her food since her dominant hand isn't fully steady enough. She coughs a couple of times, and it worries me that she's getting sick on top of everything else, but she assures us that she's okay and that the food is so tasty compared to what she's been eating at the hospital. That gets a compassionate laugh from everyone.

Aunt Ine is not quite skin and bones, but after being in the hospital for so long, she has lost some weight. At least the hollowness in her cheeks is improving since she's been home, and so is her skin tone.

After dinner, she asks me to sit out on the porch with her even though it's quite cool. My mom layers a couple of blankets over her, one for her lap and one for her shoulders. I give her one of my beanies to keep her ears warm.

"I've never been so pampered before," she teases me. "Being half immobile has its perks, I guess." But there's a quiet sadness in her voice.

"What are you thinking about?" I ask her.

She looks wistfully out at the yard. There's a smattering of fallen leaves yet to be carried away by the wind. Most of the grass has long grown patchy and is now dried up. The trees are in full-blown stick season, almost every last one of them bare. The sun is dull today, leaving the world outside in a lazy haze.

"I'm just wondering how I'd paint this place. How would I mix the yellows and tans to get the perfect ambiance?" she ponders quietly.

I'm not sure what to say, how to approach this newly sensitive topic with her. So, I stay quiet, thoughtful.

Then she continues on. "Have you drawn anything lately?"

I shake my head, but she's still looking out at the world around us. "No." Then, when I really think about it, I change my answer. "Actually," I say. "I guess I did. I made some signs for Cally's restaurant. Not my usual medium but better than the back of an order pad, I guess."

A small smile forms on my aunt's lips. "How did it feel?"

I pull the blanket up over her shoulders a little higher. "It was really nice, actually," I admit. I'd been thinking about it for a while, but it feels good to say aloud. "I had a lot of fun. I can't say I've drawn a lot of food before."

"Yeah," Aunt Ine says. "You were always good at landscapes, but you can draw anything, Travis. You're so good at capturing a person's essence in a way most people can't even see."

I think about the faces I drew on the people in the sketch I made for Cally, how I wasn't totally satisfied because it was hard to work with such a flimsy material.

"Will you take me back to my room?" Aunt Ine asks suddenly.

"Are you cold?" I ask, folding the blanket over her hands.

She shakes her head. "No. I want to get something."

I wheel my aunt back through the house. Her wheelchair barely fits through the doorways. I wonder if she'll ever be able to navigate on her own, and if she does, whether she'll be able to get around okay. Maybe we'll have to renovate her house. Or maybe my parents will have to renovate this house so she can live with them. Either way, I'm aware, probably way less than she is, that the road ahead of us is going to be tricky and full of obstacles.

Seconds after we're in her made-up room, Aunt Ine has lost her wistful look and is now looking a little more like her usual self. She points over by the dresser with her good hand. "Get that box," she says. Her eyes wrinkle in a hopeful smile.

It's a heavy wooden hand-crafted box with a few little drawers. The top has a latch that flips up to a compartment inside. It feels too weighty to put into her barely working hands, so I set in down on the corner of the bed in front of her.

She flips up the top, revealing some watercolor paper, a few small, empty glass jars, and another smaller box filled with an assortment of brushes. There's a small wooden portable easel that's folded up in a little compartment in the back. She slowly pulls out the drawers one by one, revealing rows and rows of half-used watercolors. There are four drawers and probably a hundred colors.

"I made sure your dad brought this when he went to get everything I'll need while I'm here."

"Do think you want to try it?" I ask her hesitantly. "So soon?"

She rolls her eyes at me like I've just said the most ridiculous thing and the obvious answer is staring me in the face.

She peers up at me. "I was just going to ask you that."

"Me?"

She nods affirmatively.

"But I've only used watercolors a couple of times. I don't think I—"

"Stop fighting me and take it, boy," she demands with love. "I don't want them to go to waste. You'll be doing me a favor."

A sense of foreboding rises in my chest, but I agree. "I'll take it," I say, closing the lid. "I'll think about using it. I still think it's better off in your hands, regardless."

Aunt Ine turns a little somber again, not quite sad, just different. I'm sure she's having a hard time dealing with this big change in her life. She's going to have all these limitations she's never had before.

"I think I'm going to sit in here for a bit and rest," she tells me. It's a polite dismissal, and I know she wants to be alone.

I grab the art box and plant a kiss atop my aunt's graying hair. "Yell if you need anything."

She pats my arm, and I go.

In my room, I set the art box on my desk right next to my untouched sketchpad and pencils.

I pace around for a minute before grabbing my phone. When I see I have a text from Cally, I can't help but grin. It says she hopes I'm having a good time with my family.

I miss her. It hasn't even been a full day since I last saw her, but I want to hear her voice, so I call.

At first, I think she's not going to pick up, but she answers on the sixth ring, sounding a little breathless. "Travis?"

"Hey, beautiful," I say, a smile already breaking on my face.

"How's it going? Did you guys finish your meal already?" she asks.

"Yeah, my mom even taught me how to make mashed potatoes."

She gives a cute little giggle. "Wow, you're proactive. Trying to impress me, huh?"

I join in with a hearty chuckle. "Yes, actually. That's my new goal in life." It might sound like I'm joking, but I'm pretty sure it's one hundred percent true. I wonder if she knows already. I wonder if there's a way to show her that.

"Hey! Get out of here, you little rascal. Stop trying to take my shoes!" Cally suddenly yells into the phone with a giggle. It's obvious it's not directed at me.

"Family?" I laugh.

After some shuffling and the final sound of a door closing, she's back. "Yeah." She responds with the same breathy sound as earlier. "Gotta chase these nieces and nephews around while they're still catchable. They're pretty fast already."

That launches us into an hours-long discussion about family. I don't have any siblings, and therefore, I'm not an uncle. My aunt never married, and my dad doesn't have any siblings, and my grandparents passed away when I was young. I had no cousins to play with, just my buddies like Jeremiah and Luann. She tells me all about her brother and his wife, whom he met in college in New York. She speaks fondly about her nieces and nephews. She also catches me up on what's going on with her sister, who's living her dream life as a stay-at-home mom.

We talk about what our holidays usually look like. I realize that mine have been pretty sad the last several years, whereas Cally's are always brimming with excitement.

I wonder if, next Thanksgiving, I'll be a part of that.

It's getting very dark by the time we're winding down. Cally says that she needs to go so she can give a proper goodbye to her family, so I tell her I want to see her soon and then let her go. I can sense her little blush through the phone just from the warmth in her voice when she says she can't wait.

Today, cooking alongside my mom, eating with my parents, having my aunt in attendance and getting to have a heart-to-heart with her again, and of course, talking with Cally for hours, has all

been pretty amazing. I have to say it's the most at home I've felt in…
well, maybe ever.

The realization hits me like a wave of warm summer air, fueling my lungs with life. This is it. Home.

With a flutter of inspiration at my fingertips, I open my aunt's box of painting supplies.

CHAPTER 23

Cally

THE NICE THING ABOUT THANKSGIVING IS I GET TO COOK ALL OF MY favorite recipes early in the day, but then I have the rest of the holiday to spend with my family and relax. There's no working at the Maple Falls Cafe and no waitressing when I really want to be back in the kitchen with my dad.

The kind of annoying thing about the day after Thanksgiving is that we have to get back to work at the cafe—and it's always quite busy!

One might think that an entire town who went on an all-you-can-eat marathon last weekend and stuffed their faces to their hearts' content with their families the night before wouldn't even be able to think about food for a couple of days. But well, I guess every person who lives in Maple Falls has a bottomless pit for a stomach. We are always swamped on Black Friday. It's possible it's all the shopping that makes everyone so hungry. People are already out and about, eating at our restaurant in between stops, apparently.

"I blame you for this," Jared says as he passes me with two arms full of piping hot plates. "Everyone got that sweet taste of your cooking last weekend, and they're coming back for more!"

"Oh, hush." I have to yell since the entire place is packed, and the volume is so loud, I can barely hear myself think. "My recipes aren't even on the menu. These people know that! They're looking for their favorite comfort foods."

Jared delivers the plates for two different tables and finds me a moment later. "That might be true for most folks," he says with a twinkle in his eye. "But at least five different people in the last hour have asked for a dish that was served here last weekend."

That makes me smile, but none of my recipes have made it on the menu—yet.

All day, it's nonstop work, and I'm getting swallowed up in it. Not to mention, Jared's comment has me thinking about what it would be like if I were in charge of the menu. I'm so busy tending to my tables and daydreaming about what it will be like when I run the restaurant that I don't even notice when Travis walks in.

"Excuse me, miss," he says with all the swagger of an overly-confident bachelor.

I halt at his familiar voice and laugh when I turn to find him with some kind of James Dean smolder on his handsome face, sitting on a barstool.

"When you have a minute, I'd like to place an order with you," he adds.

"Sorry, sir. This is Jared's section. You'll have to flirt with him to get what you want," I suggest nonchalantly.

He cracks a smile and then suddenly grows very serious. "But I only want to flirt with you."

As cheesy as it is, I'm just so happy to see him and have a chance to tease him. I take a millisecond break and let myself lean into him. He wraps his arm around me, holding me close.

"It's busy," he whispers.

I nod. "I'm exhausted, as you can probably tell." I gesture at my hair, which I can feel is half-falling out of its pencil bun, and I'm sure my mascara is leaking into wretched raccoon eyes.

Travis just grins and boops my nose. "All I see is your beauty."

I glare at him even though I really want to smoosh my face into his neck and squeeze him instead. "You're gonna have to pay double if my dad hears you say something like that." He chuckles.

Unfortunately, I can't afford to chat for long, so I go ahead and take Travis's order even though he's had no choice but to sit in Jared's section. Later, I deliver his food, but not before scoring his burger with a couple of ketchup and mustard hearts he may not notice beneath the bun.

Even though we talked for a while last night, and I have no doubt that he's feeling something for me, I can't help but wonder how long it will last. His aunt has been released from the hospital, and as far as I know, he still has an important presentation for work. I think I know what he wants, but I don't know what he will choose. Instead of worrying about it, though, I've decided to let myself enjoy his company and whatever time we happen to have together.

A bit later, Autumn and Lukas find a booth in my section, and between me bringing their drinks and their food, they fill me in on the news about their date for the wedding. In typical Autumn fashion, it'll be a fall wedding. I can tell they're itching to get married and start their lives together, but Autumn always envisioned a fall wedding, so they'll have to wait a while.

I'm excited to hear it, but then, when Travis slips out, leaving me with a twenty-dollar bill in an origami heart and a wink, I yearn for what Autumn and Lukas have. I want that—and I think I want it with him.

I GET OFF WORK LATER THAN EXPECTED, BUT THERE'S STILL AN HOUR OF daylight left. I walk out of the restaurant to find Travis leaning against the door of his vehicle, except it's not his rental Challenger. It's a sporty little Tacoma pickup. I don't ask questions about the change, but it does stir up some curiosity in my over-active imagination.

He greets me with open arms, which I am more than happy to run into. He gives me a tight squeeze and plants a kiss on the top of my head. My hair probably smells like smoke from the grill and fried onions, but he doesn't seem to mind.

"Wanna go see something?" he asks.

I cock my head to the side, but I answer with an extra shot of excited confidence: "Yes."

Travis opens the door like the perfect gentleman he is, and I find the inside is perfectly toasty and smells like that new car smell. I wonder if....

"I wish we were taking this drive with a little bit more daylight, but I think you'll like the destination regardless," he says, shifting the truck into reverse.

There's low, soothing jazz music playing on the radio that's conspiring with the heated seats to lull me to sleep. Travis reaches over and grabs my hand when my head starts to nod to the side.

"I know you're exhausted, but you've got to stay awake for this, sweetie," he says softly. "You'll miss the big surprise."

With the fall colors fading with the impending darkness, the drive through Maple Falls feels different. It feels mysterious to me for the first time. I'm happy to go along for the ride, and the suspense is refreshing. I truly can't guess where we're going despite knowing the exact road we're on. I've been on this route with my besties, top down on my grandpa's car and music blaring. It's the perfect summer or fall cruise. But this time, instead of continuing on through the twists and turns that will eventually lead us out of town, Travis slows his truck and flips on the turn signal.

"You awake now?" he asks.

It's clear that I am. I've perched myself on the edge of my seat, straining my eyes to see past the headlights to figure out where we could possibly be going.

He pulls into a long driveway. In the distance, a small farm-style house on a large lot with rows of various trees appears. He pulls up to the house, and its front porch light is on. The house is white with rust-colored shutters and a big front porch with nicely crafted wooden pillars.

"Where are we?" I ask, staring at him.

Without replying, Travis gets out and comes around to help me out of the vehicle. He takes my hand, leading me up to the front door.

He hasn't answered me yet, so I ask again. "Whose house is this?"

Pulling a key out of his front pocket, he unlocks the front door and pushes it open. "It's my aunt's," he says, then adds, "or rather, it's mine."

My head turns to look at him with the force of an old screen door slamming shut. "Say that again."

He laughs and runs his hands down both my arms, gleaming at me. "It's mine. She sold it to me."

"So you have a house in Maple Falls now?" I ask, completely dumbfounded.

Travis nods, keeping his eyes trained on me.

"And you have a place in Chicago... also?" I ask, just for clarification.

He shrugs. "An apartment—for now."

"For now? Are you saying... you're not going to have an apartment there—forever?"

I feel like the answer is shining right in my eyes, but I want to hear him say it.

"Cally," he murmurs, growing serious but keeping a faint smile. "I don't want to live in Chicago anymore."

"Oh, so that's why you bought the new truck? That's going to be one heck of a commute."

He gives my arms a squeeze. "Are you going to tease me this whole time?"

I suck a breath in and hold it, waiting. I shake my head, a silent promise. No more teasing. For now. "What are you saying, Travis?" I need to hear it from his mouth.

"I'm saying... I'm not giving that final presentation, the one I thought would eventually land me a seat in the CEO's chair. I don't want a job that takes up my whole life. I quit."

My heart flutters rapidly in my chest, faster than a hummingbird's wings.

"I talked with a couple of people yesterday," he continues. "I think I'm going to work for the newspaper. It's still in my field, but it'll be way less job stress and way better work hours. And, you know, I'll be way closer to you."

I'm literally speechless. This is exactly what I was hoping he would say. This whole time since he walked back into my life and I got to know him, I've wanted to stay close to him. It's a dream to hear him say that he wants to be close to me, too.

"That's a big change," I say. "Are you sure you want to do that? Move back to the town you hate?'"

"I never really hated Maple Falls," he says, sliding his fingers through mine. "I just got a little too into the details and lost sight of the big picture for a while." He leans forward and whispers, "And... I have a feeling it'll be worth it. You see... there's this girl."

He winks at me, and my knees start to cave in. "You must really like her," I manage.

With a chuckle, he says, "I'm obsessed."

My breath catches in my throat. Obsessed? Yeah... I get that.

"Travis," I say, finally lacking even the hint of a teasing thought. "I don't know what to say. I think I shouldn't be this happy, but I'm freakishly giddy right now." I wobble my knees and let the shimmy carry on through my hips and shoulders.

This elicits a rich laugh from Travis. His hands feel so at home in mine.

"What about your aunt?" I ask as soon as the question occurs to me "Where will she stay?"

"With my parents," he finishes for me. "Late last night, she admitted that even without the stroke, this place is a lot for her to take care of by herself. Now, after everything, she needs a lot of help. My mom will be her caretaker as long as she needs to be. Then, if and when Aunt Ine feels she's ready, she'll move into a smaller house in town."

"I can't believe it," I say, my mouth agape.

"There's one more thing—well, technically, two," Travis says.

He pulls me through the house so quickly I scarcely get a good look at the place. We practically race to the back, where he leads me into a large room with wide windows that look out over the land-scape behind the house. There are easels propped up all around the room and piles of paints and brushes here and there. A big writing desk cluttered with pencils and paints is pushed up against one wall.

"This is–was–my aunt's art room. You can't see much outside since it's dark, but the view is quite gorgeous from here. It overlooks the gorge at the base of the mountains."

I try to peer through the windows, but I can only see the shadowy darkness below and the outline of the trees atop the mountain with a navy blue backdrop of night sky.

"She always took me to places that inspired me. But now, I have inspiration right in front of me," he says, looking so lovingly into my eyes that I think my hummingbird heart is about to tap out and die altogether.

My mouth is dry, and my eyes are feeling misty. My extremities are numb. I'm still speechless, and all I want to do is hold him in my arms.

"Cally." Travis steps back and tugs a piece of fabric off an easel. As the cover slips away, a portrait is revealed—a portrait of me. I gasp and cover my mouth with one hand. The painting captures me perfectly on the day of the bake sale with splashes of color and a shimmer of glitter. I guess he really was committing me to memory.

I carefully place one finger on the canvas, feeling the love that was poured into the piece of art.

"I love you," I murmur.

He doesn't seem to hear me. I question whether I meant to say that out loud already. Should I say it again? I mean, I don't doubt it, so—

I spin around.

"I love you," we say in unison. And just like that, we're perfectly in sync yet again.

Travis pulls me into a tight hug. "I never want to be anywhere where you aren't." I look up at him, and his lips brush mine. Thank goodness he has his arms around me because otherwise I might collapse.

When I can finally speak again, I say, "I guess it wasn't so hard for you to quit Chicago cold turkey after all."

Without missing a beat, he says, "Easy as pumpkin pie."

CHAPTER 24

Travis

Nothing this past year has been more difficult than making sure my girlfriend is awake before 10:00 on her days off. I can stand pounding at her front door for fifteen minutes and calling her, but she doesn't wake up until I find her bedroom window and tap on it.

The first time I wanted to see her on her day off, it was past 9:00 A.M., and I had done all the aforementioned tasks. I'd been rattling her window for almost five minutes, suddenly worried about her, but it turned out she just sleeps like a rock.

Eventually, she opened the curtain, her tired little eyes squinting open in confusion. When her sleep-riddled brain processed what was going on, she opened the window, and in her adorable groggy voice, she said, "Come on in."

I was so bewildered. "What about the front door?" I asked her.

She waved me off, slinked back to the bed, and crawled into it. "Too far," she muttered.

So, I crawled in through her window on a bright December morning, tracking in snow. It wasn't graceful either, not with a giant coat and boots on. But I managed.

"You're just going back to sleep?" I asked her.

She closed her eyes purposefully and hummed.

I ended up just sitting in a chair at the foot of her bed for fifteen minutes listening to her snore lightly before taking a self-guided tour around her house until she woke up.

Somehow, this has become our strange little habit. She'll leave the window unlocked, and I'll climb in just to share a space with her. I've started bringing my sketching supplies, and she set up a little desk in the corner where I can make myself comfortable drawing until she finally gets up.

Over the last year, this has happened several times whenever we both happen to have a morning off at the same time. My girl is seriously dedicated to her sleep, but I've been thinking for a while now that I'd like to make a more permanent change in our little habit.

"Did you already set up all the tables?" Cally asks me.

Her voice is still a little sleepy. Instead of waking her up today, I let her do it on her own and just got a head start setting up for this year's craft and bake sale in the park.

I greet her with a quick kiss before removing the containers of baked goodies from her hands and setting them underneath the tent next to mine.

"Yeah. I got mine set up already so I could help you out," I tell her.

She looks adorable as ever today in a pair of red gingham pants and a pale pink sweater. It's pretty chilly, so she's wearing a long white coat, a pea green scarf, and a yellow wool bucket hat. One might not think that these colors match, but she makes them work. I love how her outfit matches her bright personality.

"You should have woken me up early so I could help you," she says.

I laugh. "No worries, beautiful. I know how important sleep is to you."

She smirks at me but doesn't disagree and then goes about setting up more of her baked goods. After a few moments, she pulls a paper bag from her coat pocket and offers it to me.

Inside, I find the same little apple pastry she gave me last year. It's still warm, and I can barely keep myself from shoving the entire treat in my mouth in one bite.

"I figured you probably hadn't eaten any breakfast." She smiles, and I nod. Cally knows me so well. I've been practicing cooking a little bit, but I'm not good at making breakfast items. Since my girlfriend and cooking teacher isn't a fan of mornings, we don't often get to spend them together. I'm hoping that will change soon.

"Thanks," I say, giving her another quick peck.

Cally peruses my booth, which is filled with dozens of original pieces that I've created over the past year. Living at the farmhouse has proven to be quite inspiring. I've finished a lot of paintings, sketches, and even watercolors. Many of them are landscapes of the gorge that my property overlooks. My work represents every season and kind of weather.

But I've also taken my Aunt Ine's advice about people. Cally is my muse, of course, but I selfishly don't want to sell any of my images of her, so I only display one, my favorite, the one I created a year ago.

"These are great," she says with a fond smile. "But my favorite is still the one hanging above my fireplace." She's talking about the scene of Chicago that I drew on her order pad that first night in the cafe with her.

"What? What about this stunning image of the love of my life? You don't like that one?" I tease, gesturing at the painting of her.

She studies it, and while she does smile, she shrugs and says, "It would be better if you were in it with me."

I chuckle and wrap her up in a hug. "Noted. I'll add myself in to the next one."

Autumn and Lukas arrive, also with armloads of goodies for Cally's tent. I've gotten to know them well over the last year, and Lukas convinced me to join his volleyball team last spring. It's actually a lot of fun. Diving after a ball or getting a solid block is thrilling in the same way I found throwing a touchdown in high school.

Then, a couple of weeks ago, I also had the pleasure of attending their wedding alongside Cally. The wedding was beautiful, but the best part was the reception. We hit the dance floor so hard. Everyone even learned the "Thriller" dance so we could do it together. It was perfect for a wedding a few days before Halloween. The two of them have just gotten back from their honeymoon, and honestly, I'm a little jealous. They keep looking at on another like the other hung the moon.

"Cally," Autumn says, sitting down some packets of cookies, "I had another dream about my wedding cake. Can you please make it again? It was so delicious, and I didn't even get a whole piece."

Cally straightens up her table. "I'll see what I can do. Maybe I'll be making one for a baby shower before too long?" She waggles her eyebrows at her friend.

Autumn laughs and tries to elbow her friend in the loving, teasing way that friends do, but packages of cookies are sliding off the edge of the table. Lukas catches a couple and quickly takes the remaining load out of Autumn's hand. "We just got married—give us some time, woman."

With a laugh, Cally says, "Sorry! I just can't wait to be an aunty."

Lukas and I leave them to chat while we focus on unloading the van. "Are you ready to be a dad?" I ask him when we make it to the van alone. I'd be lying if I didn't admit the thought had crossed my mind. A little girl with Cally's eyes...

With a smirk on his face, Lukas says, "I mean... we've talked about it. We might want to start off with something less fragile, though. Like a goldfish. Or a puppy."

I smile and slap him on the shoulder. "The two of you will make great parents when the time comes."

He smiles in thanks and inclines his head back toward the tent where the girls are chatting. "What about you? You moved here from Chicago to be with her almost a year ago. You ready to seal the deal?"

I can't contain the grin that takes over my face. All I manage to say is, "I've been thinking about it."

After a short time, we get everything unloaded and carried back to the booth. Cally's quiet friend, Ivy, who she's trying to convince me isn't really quiet when I get to know her, shows up in sawdust and paint covered overalls. "Sorry I'm late!" she says with an apologetic smile.

Autumn gets up and swipes at Ivy's pant leg. "You didn't even change this time?"

I can't help but hear the motherly tone in her voice already. Maybe Lukas does, too, because his eyes are glued to his wife.

I look at Cally, who is playing with Ivy's braids, undoing one and redoing it with lightning fast movements.

"Why are you guys fussing over me so much?" Ivy asks, flustered. "You're being weird."

Autumn and Cally look at each other cryptically, like they're sending invisible, inaudible messages through the air. Are they hoping Ivy meets someone soon? I get the impression their single friend is ready to settle down, once she finds the right guy.

The girls finish setting up Cally's booth while Lukas and I take a lap around the festival to talk about my plans... my secret surprise plans.

"Oh, my gosh, dude, that's so cheesy," Lukas says, cracking up. But before I can defend myself, he adds, "She's going to love it."

And, strangely, even though I know that's true, it's nice to hear it from someone who really knows us both. It's all the extra confidence I need to carry out my plan.

THE EVENING IS WINDING DOWN WHEN THE MAPLE FALLS SHERIFF stops by. He buys both a sketch of the town square and a couple of pumpkin pie bars from Cally before delivering us some surprising news.

"I just got through talking to your folks," he tells Cally. "We finally found out who broke into the restaurant last year."

"What?" Cally grabs for my forearm, her nails biting more than she intends. "Who…?"

The older gentleman runs a hand through his graying hair. "Well, Luann Britzen was bragging about it to someone, and my son caught wind of it. He reported it to me immediately," he says.

"Wow," I whisper. "Who did she say did it?" My friend has known the responsible party this whole time and never mentioned it? But then, I haven't exactly been spending time with her since I've returned.

Cally's eye flicker to me like I'm missing something.

The sheriff shifts. "It was her. She did it to sabotage the Harvest Feast."

I can't suppress my surprise at the news, though, come to think of it, Luann has been acting odd since I've been back in town. Cally gives me a sort of sad but pointed look, like she's not surprised at all by this news, and she's sorry that I am.

"I guess… Luann was laying it on pretty thick back then, trying to get me to go out with her," I mutter. "I told her I wasn't interested, and maybe she was trying to get back at me by attacking Cally's family's restaurant."

"So, did you bring her in for questioning or something?" Cally asks the sheriff.

He presses his lips together in a flat line. "She skipped town," he explains, turning to Cally. "I have to ask if you want to press charges. It seems like your parents are willing to let it go since there wasn't any major damage other than the door window. But I can put out a warrant—"

This is all so crazy. A warrant for Luann's arrest? That just seems unthinkable.

Cally squeezes my arm. "No, I don't think that will be necessary. I don't want to press charges."

"Are you sure?" I ask.

She looks at me and nods. "Yeah. I don't want to bother. It's been such a long time now, and besides," she says, giving me a sheepish grin. "I really enjoyed the opportunity she created for you to swoop in and save me. I'm so grateful we got to do all of that together."

The sheriff says farewell and leaves us. Cally still seems to be in a good mood, and I'm eager for Thanksgiving to come up so I can finally carry out my surprise.

CHAPTER 25

Cally

It's hard to believe it's almost Thanksgiving again! It seems like just yesterday, Travis and I were preparing the food for the town Thanksgiving feast. Now, I'm planning the meal for my family, and of course, he'll be there to help.

We've been tossing around the idea of having a joint Thanksgiving for quite a while, basically since last year. So, his aunt and parents will be joining the Steins for a gigantic Thanksgiving dinner.

Travis has been attending nearly every Stein family function since we got together last year, and I've had the pleasure of getting to know his parents. I've especially loved getting closer to his aunt. I love that he has kept his childhood nickname for her—Aunt Ine. That's so cute. She made me stop calling her Ms. Endicott, a habit it was hard to break after all these years. She insists I call her Aunt Nadine, which I absolutely love.

Travis walks in carrying a casserole dish. "What's this?" I ask. "I thought we were going to cook everything here."

He jerks it away from me like he thinks I'll devour it with my eyes.

"This one is special! I made it all by myself this morning—with my mother's guidance. I wanted to do something for you, and I think you're going to love it."

I giggle at his determination. "Okay, sweetie. Sorry," I pat him on the cheek and give him a quick kiss before opening the door wider for his aunt.

Aunt Nadine has been out of the wheelchair for a long time, but she has a bit of lingering weakness from the stroke in her right leg. She's getting around so much better, and she has even started painting again. Travis likes to take her over to her old house on the weekends, and the two of them work together all afternoon. I've joined them a few times. My art skills are pretty good, but I'm nowhere near their level, so I mostly watch and enjoy the conversation. Travis says that she's gotten stronger since being able to paint again. He thinks it has a lot to do with her mental health and motivation. I'm so happy to see them enjoying their time together doing what they love.

"Cally, it's so nice to see you," she says as she enters my parents' house. "Oh my, it smells so good in here!"

I greet her with a hug and help her out of her coat.

"Mom and Dad should be here in a little bit," Travis tells me. "Mom insisted on bringing two sides and a dessert, even though you told her it wasn't necessary."

"It's appreciated regardless," my mother says, swooping in. She catches Aunt Nadine by the arm and walks her into the living room where my brother's and sister's families are chatting and watching the parade. "Come, come. We have plenty of room. Make yourself comfortable."

"But not you, handsome." I snag Travis's elbow and pull him into the kitchen. "You're helping me, remember?"

He chuckles and follows me, balancing his mystery casserole dish on one hand. I resist the urge to take off the lid and see what's in there when he places it in the refrigerator, telling me he needs to heat it up when everything else is done. I don't want to ruin the surprise.

I've been working on ideas for recipes for months. Travis helped me perfect them. He's a great taste tester. I was able to put out some good dishes for this year's Maple Falls Harvest Feast event, but I have some specific foods I want to share with my family first. Not to mention that I'd love to impress Travis's family

Mom's turkey is taking up lots of space in the oven, so I focus, as usual, on stove-top dishes and prepping selections that can go in the oven when the turkey is done.

I love having Travis in the kitchen with me when I'm cooking. With a year's worth of practice, we're more in sync than ever. Plus, he's done his homework and studied up on the recipes so he knows what I need and when. I love every bit of the extra effort he puts in.

A couple of hours later, everything is all coming together. The turkey is out, and the mini stuffed pumpkins and pesto zucchini rosettes are in. I tell Travis to go hang out and watch the football game with the other guys while I finish up the pumpkin risotto.

"Just for a little while," he says. I can tell he's happy to hang out with my brother. They get along even better than I expected. They'd be even better friends if my brother still lived in down. "And promise you won't look at my dish?"

The more he insists that I don't look, the more curious I am. But I promise anyway and seal it with a soft kiss. "Meal's done in twenty."

He nods and runs off. Shortly after he disappears, I hear his parents arrive. His mom greets us in the kitchen and sits her contributions on the dinner table, then goes off to the living room to sit with her sister. I hear his dad cheering on the Cowboys while my brother boos.

My mom goes with to sit with the other ladies. It seems like they are also becoming good friends. I'm alone in the kitchen with the sound of water boiling and the risotto sizzling. All my favorite fragrances drift on the air like music to my nose. Every scent blends together like the perfect, comforting jazz song. I soak in the peace and gratitude of this day. Everything is perfect, better than I could have ever imagined.

Over the year, I've added several of my own dishes to the menu at the restaurant, including the maple bacon and caramelized onions pizza that Travis and I made together last year after the Harvest Feast. One of the most popular selections the mushroom and truffle oil pizza. I knew people would love pizza, and even my dad asks me to make him one for lunch at least once a week.

Dad has also allowed me to create a seasonal menu. Every two months or so, I get to create a few new dishes or bring back ones that everyone loves. And, to my surprise, it seems like Dad is actually enjoying it, too. When he decided to let go, he really basically handed over the reins. I didn't expect that at all, but I'm grateful.

The timer on the oven goes off. I'm about to open it and take out my dishes when Travis strolls up behind me, swipes the oven mitts off the counter, and does it for me. "Perfect timing!" he proclaims. "Now, I can put my dish in."

"How long does it need to go for? Should we wait to call everyone to the table?"

He slides out my dishes and swaps them for his. "That's okay. I'll just bring mine to the table when it's ready. Let's go eat. I heard Meena complaining about being hungry. Teenagers, am I right?"

I pat him on the shoulder and leave him to his business to go collect our families and get them seated at the table. My mom and Travis's mom help me put the rest of the dishes on the table while the younger kids are getting rounded up. Soon enough, we're at the table saying grace and stuffing our faces.

Everything tastes so good, and I'm sure to compliment Mrs. Thatcher on her cranberry salad and her roasted veggies. Everyone is chatting and smiling and having a good time when I hear the timer go off in the kitchen. I'm about to go get it, but Travis stops me and says he'll take care of it.

It takes him almost ten minutes to get back to the table with his dish. I am about to send a search party after him when he reappears.

"That smells good! Why didn't you bring this out sooner?" I ask him.

He shrugs. "I didn't want to show up your food."

I giggle and shake my head at him.

He has an unusual smile on his face, though, and that's starting to make me nervous. And he's looking at me in that way that seems he's memorizing every single detail, giving every inch of me all the love he holds in his heart.

"Besides," he says with a boyish smile, "this is mostly for you anyway. I want you to have the first bite."

My mom clears a space in front of me for Travis to put the dish down. He's been holding it for a while. I hope the heat hasn't permeated the oven mitts and hurt his hands.

For some odd reason, he kneels down next to me, his hand on the lid. "Are you ready?" he asks.

My heart rattles against my rib cage as my mind tries to compute what's going on. Everyone's eyes are on me—and they're all smiling.

I glance at Travis, who is waiting patiently. "Okay," I mutter. "I guess I'm ready."

He quickly pulls the lid off and sets it on the table.

My hands fly over my mouth, and I jerk my head back to him. I'm crying already.

"Well?" he asks, holding up a spoon.

I look back at his simple, beautiful little masterpiece. It's not a casserole at all, really. It's a giant pan of cheesy mashed potatoes, and some carefully placed peas spell out, "WILL U MARRY ME?"

What cracks me up is the originality of it. It's so perfectly him, finding a way to do something for me that's creative, quirky, and just… perfect.

I nod my head and press my chair out so I can sling my arms around his neck. "This is so cute. I love it, and I love you. Of course, I'll marry you," I say.

He chuckles next to my ear. "I thought you might say that, so I hid the ring in there. You have to try it to find it."

I can't help but laugh. "Oh, my gosh! Is anyone going to help me? That's a lot of food!"

He laughs too, but asks, "Is it too much? Should I fish it out for you? I put it in after I cooked it so I wouldn't damage it, and I know exactly where it is. You know, choking hazard and all."

I'm bordering on blubbering and erratic laughter. Everyone else around the table is either sniffling or giggling, waiting for my next move.

I take a look at the mashed potatoes again. There's one patch that looks a little suspiciously lumpy. I life my spoon and dig in, taking a bite from another part of the pan. The potatoes are perfectly creamy and seasoned well with salt, butter, and an array of herbs. The cheese is nice too; I can tell it's the real stuff that he hand grated, not the prepackaged shredded cheese. Then I feel it with my spoon, the hard metal of the ring.

It's a little awkward taking it out of the potatoes, but honestly, I'm here for it. This is such a unique experience. I wouldn't have it any other way. I'm about to ask for something to wipe it off, but Travis nods to my mom, who hands me a little wet wipe. I clean the ring off and take in how gorgeous it is.

"What do you think?" Travis asks. He's still kneeling next to my chair, with one hand on the table and the other on my knee, squeezing nervously.

All I can say is, "It's absolutely gorgeous."

He slides the ring on my finger. "Cally, this year has been the most amazing year of my life. I'm so blessed to have you in my life. You are so beautiful, so funny, and the best cook I've ever met. Now, I get to make you my wife, and I couldn't be happier." He has tears in his eyes when he's done speaking, and so do I.

I lean over and kiss him, and everyone at the table cheers.

"Now, let us try the potatoes," his mom says. "Cally, were they good?"

"Delicious," I say, still smiling at my fiancé.

"Thank you. I'm really glad you like them because I had to make this every week for six months to get them right." He reclaims his chair next to me, and I can't let go of his hand.

With my right hand in his, I hold up my left hand. It really is gorgeous, with a gold band and a large round diamond with a halo of opals. I've never seen anything quite like it. "It's the most beautiful ring I've ever seen in my life. It's perfect," I tell him, leaning over and resting my head on his shoulder. It's a perfect fit. And I love the way the light shines on it, the colors playing slightly differently from every angle.

"Where did you find this?" I ask.

He rubs his thumb over my knuckles. "Aunt Ine gave me the name of a jewelry maker nearby who collects vintage jewelry and also makes some of his own. This is a special request, just for you. You're unique, perfect, and special, so I wanted you to have something that reflected everything I love about you."

"Travis, you're amazing. I love you so much." I nuzzle into his neck, lost in the moment.

Then I hear Jihwan whisper, "Can we keep eating now?" and I snap out of it.

"Yes!" I say. "We don't want the turkey to get cold!"

Travis laughs and whispers in my ear, "Sometimes cold turkey is a good thing."

I meet his eyes and reply, "I couldn't agree more."

Thank you for reading! Book 3, Snowed Inn, will be out December 1, 2025. Will Ivy finally find her man?

ALSO BY ID JOHNSON

Stand Alone Titles

All I Want for Christmas is Pooch

(*sweet contemporary romance*)

Christmas Memory

(*sweet contemporary romance*)

Meet Cute Me Under the Mistletoe

(*sweet contemporary romance*)

The Doll Maker's Daughter at Christmas

(*clean romance/historical*)

Pretty Little Monster

(*young adult/suspense*)

The Journey to Normal: Our Family's Life with Autism (*nonfiction*)

Found by the Alpha (*fantasy romance*)

Sweet As Maple Syrup series

Leaving Autumn

Cold Turkey

Snowed Inn (coming Dec 1, 2025!)

Love Throughout Time

(*time travel romance*)

Back to Titanic

Back to Gettysburg

Back to Bunker Hill

Back to the Highlands

Back to Port Royal

Back to the Inquisition

Back to Salem

Back to Plymouth

Back to Whitechapel (Dec 2025)

Back to the Old West (Jan 2026)

Back to the Ton (Feb 2026)

Back to the Crown (March 2026)

Back to Pompeii (April 2026)

Silverwood Academy

(paranormal romance)

Vampire Hunter

World Builder

Realm Jumper

Celestial Springs

(psychological thriller/literary fiction/women's fiction)

Beneath the Inconstant Moon

The First Mrs. Edwards

Leaving Ginny

The Motherhood

(dystopian romance)

Rain's Rebellion

Rain's Run

Rain's Return

Ashes and Rose Petals

(contemporary romance/retelling of Romeo and Juliet and Cinderella)

Girl in the Attic

Girl From the Tomb

<u>Girl On the Beach</u>

Nashville Country Dreams

(contemporary romance)

<u>Meant to Marry Me</u>

<u>Lead Me Home</u>

<u>You Are the Reason</u>

Forever Love series

(clean romance/historical)

<u>Cordia's Will: A Civil War Story of Love and Loss</u>

<u>Cordia's Hope: A Story of Love on the Frontier</u>

The Clandestine Saga series

(paranormal romance)

<u>Transformation</u>

<u>Resurrection</u>

<u>Repercussion</u>

<u>Absolution</u>

<u>Illumination</u>

<u>Destruction</u>

<u>Annihilation</u>

<u>Obliteration</u>

<u>Termination</u>

A Vampire Hunter's Tale (based on The Clandestine Saga)

(paranormal/alternate history)

<u>Aaron</u>

<u>Jamie</u>

<u>Elliott</u>

<u>Christian</u>

The Chronicles of Cassidy (based on The Clandestine Saga)

(young adult paranormal)

So You Think Your Sister's a Vampire Hunter?

Who Wants to Be a Vampire Hunter?

How Not to Be a Vampire Hunter

My Life As a Teenage Vampire Hunter

Vampire Hunting Isn't for Morons

Vampires Bite and Other Life Lessons

Gone Guardian

Death Does Not Become Her

Blood of the Vampire Hunter (based on The Clandestine Saga)

(paranormal romance)

Night Slayer

Shadow Stalker

Queen Catcher

Mother Hunter

Father Finder

Ghosts of Southampton series

(historical romance)

Prelude

Titanic

Residuum

Lusitania

Heartwarming Holidays Sweet Romance series

(Christian/clean romance)

Melody's Christmas

Christmas Cocoa

Winter Woods

<u>Waiting On Love</u>

<u>Shamrock Hearts</u>

<u>A Blossoming Spring Romance</u>

<u>Firecracker!</u>

<u>Falling in Love</u>

<u>Thankful for You</u>

<u>Melody's Christmas Wedding</u>

<u>The New Year's Date</u>

Charles Town Brides (based on Heartwarming Holidays Sweet Romance)

(Christian/clean romance)

<u>From This Moment</u>

<u>Can't Help Falling in Love</u>

<u>It's Your Love</u>

<u>When You Say Nothing At All</u>

<u>My Girl</u>

<u>Unchained Melody</u>

<u>I Only Have Eyes For You</u>

<u>At Last</u>

<u>The Very Thought of You</u>

Reaper's Hollow

(paranormal/urban fantasy)

<u>Ruin's Lot</u>

<u>Ruin's Promise</u>

<u>Ruin's Legacy</u>

When Kings Collide

(steamy historical romance)

<u>Princess of Silence</u>

<u>Princess of Hearts</u>

Collections

<u>Ghosts of Southampton Books 0-2</u>

<u>Reaper's Hollow Books 1-3</u>

<u>The Clandestine Saga Books 1-3</u>

<u>The Chronicles of Cassidy Books 1-4</u>

<u>Celestial Springs Collection</u>

<u>Heartwarming Holidays Sweet Romance Books 1-3</u>

<u>Heartwarming Holidays Sweet Romance Books 4-7</u>

Websites: https://idjohnsonwriter.com/

Follow us on TikTok: @roguewolfpublishing

Follow on Twitter @authoridjohnson

Find me on Facebook at <u>www.facebook.com/IDJohnsonAuthor</u>

Instagram: @authoridjohnson

Follow me on Bookbub: https://www.bookbub.com/authors/id-johnson

www.ingramcontent.com/pod-product-compliance
Lightning Source LLC
Chambersburg PA
CBHW060324310726
48976CB00007B/2428